Atlas's Forbidd

Mystic Wolves 7
Elle Boon

By Elle Boon elleboon@yahoo.com

Atlas's Forbidden Wolf
    Mystic Wolves 7
    Copyright © 2019 Elle Boon
    First E-book Publication: 2019
    Cover design by Valerie Tibbs
    Edited by: Tracy Roelle
    All cover art and logo copyright © Valerie Tibbs of Tibbs Design

    PUBLISHER:
    Elle Boon

Dedication

With each story I write I seem to find out a little more about myself. With Atlas's and Joni's story, I'm learning to embrace all my imperfections, and trust me...there are a lot of them. You see, I don't like changes, at all. However, some changes you just can't stop, like your kids growing up and becoming adults. My Goob, my baby boy is graduating high school and is actually going away to university. For me, this is a change I kinda knew would probably happen, but I sort of pretended like it was a long way off, until BAM, it is right here and now. I hope you read this story, and maybe take a look back at all the others and see if you can find all the little bits of me in them, cause yep, they're in there hidden like little Easter eggs.

I'd like to dedicate this book to all my friends who think they're less than. None of us are perfect, but lets face it, if we were, we'd all be a bunch of plastic people nobody would really like (Or at least that's my story and I'm sticking to it). I'm in my mid to upper forties, and I'm still learning to love myself. I hope as you follow Joni's journey to find love and acceptance outside her little bubble, you fall in love with these two different characters as much as I did.

Love yourself first and foremost, then you'll find the ability to love others easier.

Love y'all so hard
Elle

Other Books by Elle Boon

Ravens of War
Selena's Men
Two For Tamara
Jaklyn's Saviors
Kira's Warriors

Mystic Wolves
Accidentally Wolf & His Perfect Wolf (1 Volume)
Jett's Wild Wolf
Bronx's Wounded Wolf
A Fey's Wolf
Their Wicked Wolf
Atlas's Forbidden Wolf

SmokeJumpers
FireStarter
Berserker's Rage
A SmokeJumpers Christmas
Mind Bender, Coming Soon

Iron Wolves MC
Lyric's Accidental Mate
Xan's Feisty Mate
Kellen's Tempting Mate
Slater's Enchanted Mate
Dark Lovers
Bodhi's Synful Mate
Turo's Fated Mate
Arynn's Chosen Mate
Coti's Unclaimed Mate

Miami Nights
Miami Inferno
Rescuing Miami

Standalone
Wild and Dirty
SEAL Team Phantom Series
Delta Salvation
Delta Recon
Delta Rogue
Delta Redemption
Mission Saving Shayna
Protecting Teagan
The Dark Legacy Series
Dark Embrace

Chapter One

Joni's senses were on high alert. She'd bought the little Toyota Celica because it got great gas mileage; it would run forever, and it was the absolute last vehicle anyone would think she'd own. Plus, it was cute and sporty. She considered that a win since not much else had been a winner in her world as of late. The last time she'd seen Sky and Taryn she'd fled like a scared little wolf, but at the time she'd been so excited to feel her wolf come forward, taking over and allowing her a chance to escape before Jett could make her stay. If she'd known it would've been the last time she might have ran for days instead of hours. Of course, she had been getting used to her new non-shifting since Keith had totally screwed up her world. At least now that she wasn't going to have to face anyone from her pack she wouldn't have to lie or pretend.

Shoot, she was doing it. She was leaving her latest pack, the Mystic Wolves. Well, it wasn't like she'd had a lot of packs to call her own, only two, but still...she was going lone wolf. The thought made her stomach flip and her wolf howl. "Shut it, you little bitch," she muttered and reached under the front fender for the extra key to the car. She'd been planning her escape from the pack for a long time. Although, to be fair, the Mystic Pack wasn't bad. To be honest, if things had been different, if she'd been different, she might have loved it. However, she wasn't different. She was the little wolf who allowed Keith to experiment on her after he mentally tortured her. All so that she could help her friend, in silence.

"There's no use crying over things we can't change, so buck up." The key slid into the driver's door, unlocking the little sporty vehicle. She settled into the leather seat, exhaling loudly at the cold that met her bare legs. Damn, she probably should've thought of different clothes when she'd shifted. Her pity party didn't call for warm clothes though, she reminded herself. The memory of why she'd been dressed in one of her favorite little dresses made her heart ache. Damn Atlas and his sweet sexy bear self. She'd been so sure he was it for her. Her wolf had even whined and rolled over for him. Oh, she hadn't allowed him to fuck or make love to her. No, Joni was saving that for her mate. Of course, Taryn and Sky didn't know that. Or maybe they did. But she'd given him her heart. She'd lost a piece of herself when he walked away.

"Enough, Joni. Get the hell outta town, girl." She put her seatbelt on, then twisted the key. The soft purr of the engine reassured her she hadn't bought a lemon. At least she'd done something right. If only Atlas wasn't a bear, promised to marry another bear. Stupid bear politics. Just because his family was richer than sin, they expected him to mate some perfect six foot bear bitch and make perfect bear cubs. Goddess, she sounded like a twat, and she was not a twat.

She'd told him she wished him well, and she almost meant it. Even when regret had shown in his chocolate brown eyes, she'd wished him a happy mating and lots of adorable cubs. However, the thought of him making love to someone other than her made her wolf want to claw the unknown woman's eyes out. Unwise, because a bear and wolf fight would only have one outcome, unless it was one bear against a pack of wolves. Her pack, or rather the only people she'd considered hers, were now happily mated with hunky male wolves, while she was left on the outside looking in. The status of her entire life seemed to always be of an outsider.

She swiped at the tears the realization caused, promising she'd find happiness or die trying.

Joni flowed into the strangely busy traffic on the highway, heading South. Bears lived North, so she was heading South. Warm weather where lots of humans lived. This time next week, she'd be sipping daiquiris on a beach with a tan. That's her plan, and she's sticking to it, if only her heart didn't ache at the loss of her friends, what she knew would've been her mate. Either she'd have to settle for a loveless, or matingless relationship, or she stayed single. "I should get stock in batteries. I should also stop talking to myself, if I don't want people to think

I'm crazy." Keeping her wolf repressed was sure to make her a little unhinged, but what other choice did she have?

Hours later, tiredness pulled at her, making the highway appear a little blurry. The songs she'd downloaded to her playlist were getting on her nerves. She tapped the steering wheel to one of the rock songs she now knew word for word. Sylar and their song Shook had her screaming along to the lyrics while her body seemed to bop to the beat. The lyrics 'You can talk the talk while we walk it' resonated within her. The ones who should've always had her back didn't. They paid lip service when it suited them, but when the chips were down, the only one she'd been able to count on was herself. Of course, her two best friends couldn't be blamed. Hell, both Sky and Taryn had suffered more than any should, which made Joni that much more of an outsider because she'd been mostly unharmed. Her parents were weak, caring only to please a bastard alpha, until he was killed, freeing them all from the chains he'd bound them with.

A sign for the next town appeared on the lonely stretch of highway. The little symbols below showed her there were hotels, restaurants, and gas stations. Her fuel gauge glared at her, or maybe that was her inner self with a reminder that she was getting down to a quarter tank. If she'd learned anything from too many close calls within her old pack, it was to never allow her car to get too much below that, especially with night closing in and nobody but herself to contact for help. Nope, she'd be stopping for gas first, then decide if Oklahoma City suited her for the night. With close to five hundred thousand people, nobody would pay her any mind. After the first couple hours, she'd started looking out for signs that told how many residents each city had. Why, she had no clue. It was her minds way of staying busy and the need to focus on something other than her shit of an existence as the miles flew by.

Her little car bumped over the small speed deterrents as she steered toward an open pump. "Wow, this place is happening," she muttered. Several people turned to stare at her when she stopped, making her cringe. It dawned on her that her radio was blaring at such a level even those who were outside could probably hear perfectly. Not wanting to draw too much attention to herself, she quickly turned the volume down, then shut the engine off. Several sets of eyes continued to glare at her. She almost gave them the bird, but self-preservation kept her in check.

Before she could change her mind, she got out, shocked to see a prepay only sign on all the pumps. "Shoot," she growled. Reaching back inside her car, she pulled her purse out. Having the smarts to withdraw plenty of cash prior to setting out, she walked toward the door. The feeling of being watched continued while she grabbed a bottle of flavored water and a candy bar. Her hips definitely didn't need the extra calories from the chocolate goodness, but she didn't care. At the counter, she also grabbed a pack of gum and waited for the cashier to come over.

Joni looked to where the female was talking animatedly on a cellphone. A minute passed, and still the young girl didn't stop talking, or giggling. "Excuse me, miss, can I pay for these and prepay for my gas?"

The human glared at her. Her eyes roamed from Joni's head to where the counter hid her. If Taryn had been with her, she'd have given the girl a look that would've shriveled just about everyone. Joni didn't have the backbone like T or Sky. Nope, she'd just stand there and let the girl look, but she wouldn't look away, meeting dull blue eyes with her own. As the moment drew out, Joni's wolf raked at her to come out.

"Hold on a sec, Tyler, I gotta ring some lady's stuff up." She moved to the register. "Anything else?" she asked after scanning the food and drink.

"Yeah, I need thirty dollars' worth of premium unleaded." Pride had her standing taller. "If I can't put that much in my tank, do I come back for a refund?"

With an eyeroll any teen would appreciate, the young girl took a deep breath. "Yeah, just come on back."

Joni accepted her receipt, saying thanks in a dry tone, and then left before she did something stupid, like grab the girl by her ponytail and smack her. Nope, she wasn't going to do anything senseless that would draw even more attention to herself. From here on out, she'd make sure her radio was down and find only stations that took a card at the pump.

The girl's slight twang followed Joni out the door. Her 'Bye y'all, come back now real soon,' didn't give Joni the sense she meant it, which was fine by her.

Once at the pump, she decided to throwaway some of the trash she'd accumulated in her over twelve hour road trip so far, while the gas poured into her tank.

The constant staring was getting on her last nerve. She'd wonder if it was her eyes that had people staring, but the two different shades weren't easy to see at night.

Once the pump clicked off, she made short work of righting the thing and got into her car. "Clearly, I underestimated my fuel." Before she left, she watched the gauge move to the almost full mark, making her exhale in relief. The last place she wanted to return was inside with the attitude girl. Nope, she needed a place to sleep with a working shower before she'd head out again. Yes, most people would've told her she was crazy driving so long alone in a day, but the need to put as much distance between herself and Sturgis kept her going forward. Only because the road was beginning to get blurry did she stop, otherwise she'd have continued on through the night. "Now, which hotel was the question." She strummed her fingers on the wheel while the light was red, looking left and right, her options were pretty great. Again, she chose the right side, which maybe she should've rethought, but the parking lot looked full, so she prayed she would get in and out without much notice.

Of course, luck wasn't on her side as she stepped through the door, only to come to a hard stop. The large space was clean and everything a chain hotel would have, but this one seemed to be holding a convention for *hot guys are us*, or some shit. With her shoulders back, her eyes trained on the front desk, she moved into the line with the others trying to get a room. Dammit, she totally should have gone left. Too late to turn back, she pulled her phone out and pretended to be engrossed in whatever was on her screen.

"Ah, looking up lyrics to your favorite song?" a deep voice asked from way too close to her wolf's liking.

Joni raised her head slowly, meeting a laughing gaze staring back at her. "Something like that," she agreed. The song Figures by Jessie Reyez was almost like a script from her life. She'd surely given Atlas a ride or die and he gave her games. She'd given him her all, getting shit in return. Yeah, Figures was her latest jam. Maybe she should switch to some death metal where she was singing along to a chorus that had more head banging, and less wordy shit?

"I prefer to hum along to songs. Keeps me from making a fool of myself." The man grinned at her, like he expected her to return it, or engage him. Nope, she was done with men for a while. Her heart needed to heal while she grew a freaking backbone and a will of steel.

Not wanting to encourage further conversation, she just nodded, looking down at her phone, pressing on the mail icon. A quick peek over her shoulder made her rethink her decision. No way did she want anyone getting a glimpse at her personal shit. Fucking men, she groaned inward.

Finally, it was her turn at the counter. She sighed in relief as she moved forward, putting space between her and Creepy McCreepy. Okay, she may be thinking too harshly about the poor bastard, but damn, can't a woman stand in a line without someone looking over their shoulder?

"How can I help you?"

Joni blinked slowly. Hello, she was in line at a hotel. Wasn't that a clear indication of what she wanted? She chastised her inner bitch, then snorted. "Sorry, I'd like a room please."

While she was told what was available, Joni kept her focus straight ahead. "A king would be great," she said.

"Fantastic. How many in your party?"

"Me and my fiancé." No way in hell was she announcing to the room at large she was all alone.

The clerk slid the key cards that were tucked into a small paper pouch to her. "Breakfast is free, but I'd suggest coming down early instead of waiting closer to the end time. We've got a baseball tournament in town."

Nodding, she took the keys. "Thank you," she said, without agreeing to her suggestion. There had been several fast food chains on the same street, which was where she planned to grab a quick breakfast before heading out. More than likely, like the last three meals she'd eaten, breakfast would be scarfed down while she drove.

"Hey, a bunch of us are going to the bar for drinks. You're welcome to join us."

Joni stared at the man who she'd named Creepy. At five foot seven, she wasn't the tallest or shortest woman, average was what she'd been called by her parents. The man in front of her was a few inches taller than she was, but not nearly as tall as Atlas. However, most men weren't as tall or built like her ex. His huge size was due to the fact he was a bear. The human male in front of her didn't even stack up against her image of Atlas. Not many men, human or shifter could. Of course, if she was wanting the polar opposite of what she'd had, this guy would fit the bill. Lean and muscular instead of big and brawny. Her wolf snarled in her head. "Thanks for the offer, but I'm whipped."

"You can bring your guy, too. Oh, I'm Chuck by the way." He held out his hand.

For the first time, Joni took in his complete appearance. She'd bet her last dollar he was part of one of the ball teams, maybe one of their top players. His perfectly styled hair along with his good old boy grin said he was used to getting what he wanted. Sorry to be the one to break his streak. She shook her head, avoiding his hand. "Thanks anyway, but I need to give my fiancé a call and let him know where we're staying." She held her phone up with a blessedly blank screen this time.

Chuck sighed. "Well, if you change your mind, we'll be in there." He pointed behind him to where the bar clearly was, if the low hum of country music was anything to go by.

Her phone ringing kept her from having to answer Chuck. She waved without looking at him again. The number on the display wasn't one she recognized, but she needed to keep up the farce of having a boyfriend. Gah, she hated lying, knew her face turned beet red when she did.

"Hi," she answered cheerfully like she'd known who was on the other end.

"Where the hell are you?" a familiar male voice growled.

She closed her eyes and prayed for patience. Her father only spoke to her when she did something wrong, or he needed her help. They were geniuses, but so was she. The only ones in the pack who knew just how smart she was, were her parents. They'd said it kept her safe. Only she thought it was so they could take credit for things she'd done. Which was fine. It really was, she swore to herself while her wolf whined. "I'm so happy to hear your voice," she said a little too loud, keeping up the happy appearance until she was shut inside the elevator.

"Are you sassing me, Joni Stark?" Her father's tone went lower, showing his inner wolf was pushing forward.

Her parents used her full name when they were angry, disappointed, and when she'd done what they couldn't. They were tech savages. Literally savages when it came to anything electronic. It had been thanks to them that their old pack had as much money as they did. With both her mom and dad hacking into accounts, taking money from the rich who wouldn't miss the money, while they used it to make more. They'd always been one step ahead of being caught, filling the asshole Keith, their old alpha's coffers. "What do you need, father?" she snarled.

"I asked where you were?" he said in an even tone.

"And I didn't answer you." Her mind froze when she thought of their ability to track her. Shit, in her need to flee, she hadn't considered anyone looking for her.

"Let me ask you another question, then. Why did you withdraw all the funds in the family account?" His voice turned deadly.

Joni pulled the phone away from her ear, then put it back. "First of all, it's none of your business. Second, or maybe first, the money wasn't the family's money, it was mine. Third, and goddess I hope last thing I have to ask, is how'd you find out?" She'd set up her own account when she turned eighteen, seven years ago. Unlike her parents, she didn't steal from Peter to pay Paul, then turn around and pay Peter back with their ill gotten gains. She may not have a degree from a prestigious college, but she had one she'd been able to get while doing classes online. Keith had known she was smart since her parents had allowed her the freedom.

"Don't take that tone with me. What're you doing, footing the bill for your bear?"

Oh, he thought she'd only get a mate if she paid for one? She wanted to laugh and tell them just how wrong they were. Atlas was rich as fuck and was slated to be alpha of his clan. She didn't say any of that, knowing they'd take pleasure in realizing he'd dumped her after she gave him her everything. Goddess, she was stupid. Hot tears burned her eyes, which she swiped at as the doors opened on her floor. "I'm not footing the bill for anyone, let alone Atlas, thank you very fucking much." She hung up before he could react, turning her phone off. How he'd gotten her digits, she didn't know, but come first thing tomorrow, she'd have one of those pay as you go cellphones.

Hell, her heart beat erratically against her chest at the thought she could've been followed. "I'm a big girl. I can do what I want," she mumbled. Pushing the heavy door open, she entered the room she'd rented. The newer looking furniture met her standards, like the bed, which was piled with pillows. Her backpack slipped off her shoulder while she kicked off the shoes she'd worn for the drive. When she'd decided to leave Mystic, cutting off her only family and friends, she'd also left most of her possessions. A new beginning, one where she wasn't looked at like she was nothing.

The bathroom had all the things she'd need in the morning when she decided to shower. For tonight, she was going to fall into bed and let her dreams take her away.

Her shorts landed next to the backpack, followed by her bra. In nothing but her T-shirt and panties, she crawled under the covers, shivering at the cool material against her skin. She prayed like hell that no dreams of what could've been would infiltrate her mind while she slept.

Atlas wasn't happy. His bear was furious. Neither of them wanted to be where he was driving to, knowing what he had to face. Driving through the town his clan called home, he stared straight ahead, while the ones who recognized his pearl white Escalade were already calling ahead to let them know he was home. "Fucking grapevine at its finest," he growled. Home, the word even sounded like shit in his mind. For over three hundred years, the White Bear Clan had ruled their little town and everyone in it. Now, it was his turn to take the mantle as alpha, solidifying the fractured pack with a mating. Normally, he'd be elated to return to the clan after a long absence, but this time, the only thing he felt was a sense of loss. "Fuck, this ain't what I want," he growled. What he'd wanted was a curvy little wolf shifter who fit him in every way. Just how perfect she would be when they would finally come together was something he'd dreamt about.

He gripped the leather wheel with one hand, the knuckles almost white with the death grip he had on it. An overwhelming urge to turn back, to go back toward Mystic where he'd left his heart and soul, grew stronger with each second, each mile, he put between them. Goddess, Joni Stark was his Fated truemate. Their souls, it didn't matter they were different species, had connected, assuring him she was his just as he was hers. Only he had to destroy her in order to leave, or she'd have a clan of angry bears tracking her with one goal; to kill her, end her so that he'd do his duty for the clan. His bear growled, wanting the little she-wolf as much as he did but knowing they did the only thing they could to save her.

With his free hand, he stabbed at the touchscreen of his radio, letting the heavy rock music fill the small space. "Fucking archaic rules. When I'm alpha, I'll be making a shitton of changes, one of the first being outdated laws that forced a mating."

The time on the dash assured him he'd be making the deadline he'd been given by the clan leader, not that she'd given him any choice. *"Come home and mate with the girl, or we come to you and rain hell down on that mangy pack."* The angry words reverberated around his mind at the memory. Oh, he didn't doubt for a second she'd order something like that. The only reason he hadn't told her to go fuck herself was an image of Joni lying lifeless beneath one of the female grizzlies who would love to hurt him. He'd not found his one within their tiny town, which was one of the reasons he'd set out, to look for *her*. Having clan business gave him the perfect escape, which he'd been doing for the last five years. Never, not once in all that time had it been mentioned that he'd been paired to a female he'd never met. Who the hell was the girl named Clementine, and what damn clan was she from? He had visited every clan he'd known, and not once had he met a female of mating age with that name.

The alpha estate driveway was the next turn, but his bear and he weren't ready. He looked at the time, gauging he had another couple of hours, time he wanted with his own family. Not that they were the loving kind, but at least he could look at those who had a small familial tie to him before he took the reigns as alpha.

Without pausing, he passed the first turnoff, taking the one that would lead to where he'd grown up, the one where he'd been the odd bear out because he hadn't looked like the other grizzlies. They thought he was weak, something to be put down, until they'd tried. Atlas taught them the error of their ways when he'd been barely older than a cub, taking down not only his own father, the alpha, but then the biggest enforcer of the clan. At only seven winters, he'd instilled fear and a prophecy come true. The white grizzly would become the alpha to lead them into the future, but he was to do it by mating with a female of another clan, uniting them. What clan hadn't been shown, but the time was ticking.

As his Escalade slid to a stop, the door to the cabin opened, showing the immaculate visage of his mother still looking as beautiful as she'd been when he was a cub. Only her cold brown eyes showed her hatred for him. He still didn't understand why she'd always hated him, other than he wasn't like her other cubs. His sister shoved past their mother, a wide grin on her face when she saw him, making him smile back. No matter how much his mother hated him, he could always count on his sister Shauny's love and acceptance, like his brothers, who also accepted him, much to their mother's dismay. They not only cared for him, they loved him like family were meant to. Abyle and Atika were twins, older by two years, yet smaller than him. Both men ambled out from the barn, their flannel shirts open as if they'd recently shifted and hadn't had time to fully dress. He raised one hand from the wheel, giving them a small wave in greeting at their nods.

"Well, you gonna sit in there all day or what?" Shauny asked, her hands on hips encased in denim that fit her curves while she yelled from outside his driver's side door.

Atlas shook his head, pushing the button to turn the engine off. The silence was almost deafening. He pocketed the fob before getting out, leaving his bag inside, knowing he didn't have a lot of time to visit, not that his mother looked real inviting to begin with. "Hello, squirt. I see you didn't get much taller since I saw you last," he joked, rubbing the top of her head with his knuckles.

Shauny swatted at his arm, laughter falling from her easily regardless of the fact their mother was glaring daggers at the both of them. "I'll have you know I'm now the tallest female in the clan," she said.

Atlas looked down, noticing, not for the first time, how gorgeous his baby sister was. His eyes met the twins over her head. "We're gonna need to have a talk with the clan."

Atika's lip lifted in a grin. "You're gonna be alpha shortly. No need to talk to the clan, just make an alpha order."

Abyle lifted his hand. "I'll second the motion."

Their little sister narrowed her eyes. "If you three are talking about me, I suggest you forget whatever insanity you're coming up with. For one thing, I'm not interested in any of the males around here. Second, I have zero interest in any males...at this time. Third, when I do decide it's time to mate up, I'll be choosing who, what, where, and when, not the lot of you." With each point she held up a finger until her voice was a near rumble.

"Shauny, I need you in the kitchen. Since I didn't know you'd be stopping by for dinner, I'll need to add some extra to feed you, Atlas." His mother's tone suggested she'd rather chew broken glass and gargle with cat piss.

With a shake of his head and a hand on Shauny's arm, he sighed. "I'm not going to be here long enough for dinner, Sonya." He hadn't called her mom, mother, or anything other than her given name since he'd been a cub. The memory of the day he'd found his father lying in the snow, red staining the white, was so ingrained in his mind it still made his bear agitated. His mother and her cold brown eyes had stared at him while he'd struggled to bring his father's body home, blame written on her face. He gave a mental brake pump and focused on the present.

"Home for less than an hour, but already your heading back out on your quest for a truemate?" she scoffed.

Atika growled, the warning clear in the deep baritone. "Watch your tone, mother."

"Easy, brother." No matter how much he disliked the woman who birthed him, he didn't want to cause a fight between his brothers and her. "I'm due at the alpha estate to claim my title. I assumed you'd been told." He looked to Abyle then Atika, finally settled on Shauny, knowing his sister would've been up on all the gossip if it had been spoken as if it was a big deal. The fact none of his family seemed to be aware had his bear raking at his insides. Fucking hell.

"Give us ten minutes; we're coming with you." Atika, the older of the twins didn't give him a chance to agree or disagree before he turned and strode back toward the barn where he and Abyle's home was located.

"I'm coming too," Shauny said.

"You'll do no such thing," Sonya growled, her bear clearly near the surface.

Shauny marched up the porch steps, looming over the matriarch of the family. "My brother, your son, is being made alpha today. His family should be there. Hell, he'll be in charge of the entire clan, making laws and all that which his father did before him. If you were smart, you'd be coming as well."

Her words were a reminder that their mother had mated with another after their father's murder, a grizzly who cared for nobody but himself, and the woman he'd claimed, Sonya ex-mate to the alpha of the White Bear Clan. He hated all three of her sons, but never let anyone see just how much, except his loving mate. How a mother could allow a male to treat her children the way he had was a mystery none of them knew. When Brock had been shot by a human hunter, his skin stripped off his bear form while his body was left for them to find, nobody but Sonya had wept. Luckily, Shauny had been an infant and didn't know the man or how he'd been.

"Don't think to tell me what to do in my own home, little girl. Just because you've gotten a little too big for your britches don't mean I won't knock you down a peg or ten," their mother warned, her right hand flexing.

Over his dead fucking body would he allow the bitch to lay a hand on his baby sister. She'd put more scars on him than he cared to count or remember, but he wouldn't stand for one claw to touch Shauny. "I wouldn't if I were you," he said in a deadly whisper, somehow finding himself at the bottom of the steps.

Cold, fathomless brown eyes stared at him. "Don't think I'll be celebrating when you take your father's place as alpha. He'd be alive if it wasn't for you," she spat.

Atlas nodded. "I didn't expect you to be there, Sonya Kincaid." He used the last name of her latest mate, not his father's, not the legacy his father had left them with. No, the female who had birthed him was nothing but that, a female who'd birthed him. "Go on, Shauny, I'll wait here for you." The unsaid warning clear. He'd know if anything happened to his baby sister while she gathered her things to go with him.

Shauny stepped away, then hurried through the door. The loud bang as the screen shut behind her echoed. For a few more seconds, he and his mother stared at one another until she finally turned and followed his sister inside. He didn't breathe easily until his sister returned.

Chapter Two

Joni woke drenched in sweat, nightmares from what Keith had made her suffer plaguing her throughout her dreams. The time on her phone showed she'd managed a solid five hours which was her norm. A quick shower, and then she'd jump on the road again. This town was not her end destination. The way the locals had stared at her let her know they were not the most welcoming of peeps. It wasn't that she was that odd, but clearly they didn't appreciate her all black attire and straight black hair. Maybe she looked too much like the girl from the movie the Ring, only the grown up version. Hell, there were many days she felt like her.

Shaking off her morbid thoughts, she got out of bed, showered and dressed in all black as usual, and avoided looking in the mirror as she left her wet hair to dry on its own. A sheet of paper by the door showed her fees for the night with the amount owed already paid, which of course she'd done when she checked in with cash. She looked back at the small room, making sure she hadn't left anything behind, then walked out the door. Her senses didn't pick up anything. Of course, her wolf was in hiding, which was her new normal, the pussy. Keith had beat her down mentally to where she couldn't get the animal to come out, even now after the bastard was dead. "I fucking hate him," she growled, the human version having less heat.

"Excuse me, young lady, watch your language. There are children around," a woman with two small children snapped near the elevator.

Joni bit her lip on a sharp retort as she stared at the human, noticing her shirt had a skeletal hand with the middle finger sticking up on it. "Sorry, I didn't see you there." Joni grabbed her long wet hair, twisting it into a messy bun on top of her head while they waited for the elevator, not saying another word. She could feel three sets of eyes on her as she stood there, staring at nothing. Finally, when she was sure the elevator had to be broken, she took a step back, her intent to take the stairs, when one of the kids raised his hand.

"Was you in the Transformers movies?"

His question caught Joni off guard. "Um, what?"

The woman Joni assumed was the mother put her hand over his mouth. "Charlie, of course she's not Megan Fox." Her sneer was enough to let Joni know she found her lacking in many areas.

"Your grandma's right, I'm not her, but thank you for the compliment, Charlie," Joni responded. Her little dig hitting home as the elevator doors slid open on a silent swish.

While the woman ushered her kids inside, Joni followed, keeping her smile from showing on her face.

"I'm their mother, not their...their grandmother, I'll have you know. Of course, children tend to have issues with telling ages."

Again, Joni could hear the sneer, but didn't let it go. "Oh, I wouldn't know. I'm twenty-five and tend to not judge a person by their age, but by how they act, especially toward others." She shrugged, making her leather backpack almost slip off her shoulder as she did so.

"Hey, mom, she's only a couple years younger than you are," the other kid shouted.

Luckily for all of them, the door opened on the main floor, allowing the mother and her kids to escape before she could be embarrassed further, or possibly before she could release another volley of rudeness, to which Joni would have to cut her back, verbally of course. Goddess, she hated snooty bitches and really wished her wolf would come out just a little so she could smack her down with a paw. Or not. Shit, she really was as useless to a pack as a human was. Good thing she'd left the Mystic Wolves, or she'd have proven to them all just how fucked up she was, thanks to what Keith had done to her.

She'd thought being with Atlas, a bear shifter, would've been good for her. He was an apex predator who didn't seem to care whether she shifted or not, and since he didn't have a pack to judge her, Joni had been positive they were perfect for one another. If she was being honest, she'd hoped his bear would've scared her into changing. However, he never shifted in front of her, then he up and left. She'd felt a connection to him like she'd never had for anyone else and was sure he had felt the same. When she'd seen a golden trail linking them, one like she'd seen between the mated pairs, she'd been sure it was the same for them. Clearly she'd been wrong, again.

Like the night before, conversation stilled as she walked out of the elevator following the mother and her kids. In that moment, she wished she had the courage of her friend Taryn. She'd have raised both middle fingers and flipped them all off. Instead, she kept her eyes forward, her shoulders kinda back, and continued walking out the door without looking back. Stupid humans and their ignorance. Her ears picked up murmurs of conversations, a kid yelling excitedly that he was sure she was in his favorite movie and wished he'd gotten her autograph.

Joni opened the door to her car, snorting. If she'd been a movie star, she'd definitely have a higher end vehicle. Her backpack landed on the passenger seat before she got into the driver's, the leather creaking as she settled into it, then she was off and back on the road, looking for a fast food place to grab a quick breakfast. No way was she going to get out and deal with more stares.

A few hours later, she saw a sign for a town called Wolf's Run and felt a certain pull toward it, almost as if that was where she was meant to go. A glance at her gas gauge assured her she needed to stop for fuel, which in her mind was another reason for her to stop and test her senses. She was a wolf, a wolf in hiding within her body, but a wolf. Surely, a town with that name had to mean something in a karma sort of way. Not that she thought real wolves like her would be stupid enough to settle in an area with such a name. Wolves were way smarter than that, but she believed the Goddess guided them and felt a pull, even though her last one had told her Atlas was something other than just a sexy male shifter. "Enough feeling sorry for yourself, Jonigirl," she chastised herself, taking the first exit that showed there were several gas and food options on the turn off.

Before she'd decided to take off, she'd been smart and created a new identity. Her parents, along with Joni herself, had been the tech geeks for Keith and his pack. She wasn't sure when she'd realized she could actually surf the web mentally, using more than the average ten percent of the human brain. She'd tried to examine herself as she'd looked on, comparing what she knew about the human brain, and that of most shifters, but nothing was exactly the same. In the end, she gave up, thinking her brain was about forty to fifty percent while most shifters were on average twenty to twenty-five percent. What that meant she wasn't one hundred percent positive, only knew she could manipulate many electronics, including fabricating documents, which was how she had a new identity that was as authentic as anyone else's. Joni, for all intents and purposes was no longer. "Hello, my name is Vanessa," she said, testing the name.

She'd have changed her appearance, but shifters had a hard time altering anything about themselves unless she wanted to wear a wig. If she'd have gone north, it wouldn't have been too hard, but south with the heat, there was no way she'd have been able to wear one without constantly itching. Nope, she figured nobody would really search for her since she had—well, the reality of her situation was, nobody cared enough to miss her, to even come looking for her. Maybe Taryn and Sky, but they had mates now. After a couple weeks pass, Joni planned to hack into a phone system and give them a call. If for no other reason than to reassure them all was well.

The first gas station was packed full of cars, which meant a lot of prying eyes, so she kept driving. Two blocks down, she found a smaller station with several open pumps that she eased her little car into. Her legs protested when she stood up, clearly not happy being cramped inside a vehicle for so long. She inhaled deeply, trying to scent whether or not anything smelled wrong, but the only thing that assaulted her senses was gas and deep fried food, which instantly made her stomach growl.

After fueling up the gas tank, she went inside and paid, then looked around for a few snacks just in case she decided not to stick around. The older woman at the counter smiled sweetly, her warm brown eyes crinkling at the corners while she rang up her gas. "Hello, you're not from around here, are ya?"

Joni shook her head but smiled back. "Nope, I was passing through, but saw the name of the town and thought it looked like a nice place to stop for a bit."

A laugh bubbled out of the woman, making her entire body shake. "Yeah, the old...settlers who came here first had a wonderful sense of humor they say. So, where you heading?"

Joni thought it odd the familiar way she spoke, but the woman seemed friendly enough. "Not too sure, yet. I'm sort of on a journey of self-discovery." She ducked her head, tucking her hair behind her ear, a nervous habit she'd tried to break but didn't seem to be able to do even though Keith had nearly bitten it off more than once. She'd hidden the scars from his bites with jewelry she'd created that shifted with her until her wolf decided to stop coming out.

"Oh, those are lovely," the woman said, her hand reaching across the counter.

Joni covered her ear, hiding the ear and the jewelry.

"Annie, you bothering the customers again?"

A giant of a man asked, coming to stand behind the woman called Annie. His thick hair was mostly grey, but his eyes were sharp, his voice deep but kind.

Joni took a step back, her eyes darting toward the door. "Thank you for the gas and the compliment. I...I'll just be leaving," she stammered.

"Now see what you did, Hollis. You've gone and scared my new friend. I'm sorry, I didn't catch your name, sweetheart?"

Joni bit her lip, not wanting to hurt the nice lady's feelings and tell her it was because she didn't throw it at her. "Vanessa. My name's Vanessa," she lied. Well, her new identification said that was her name, so technically, that was her name.

Hollis's eyes narrowed, but he held out his hand. "Sorry if I scared you, little bit. My Annie doesn't usually take to customers very well. You just passing through or you looking to stick around for a while?"

Joni wasn't sure why he was asking her so many questions. Heck, the man kind of reminded her of Emerson, or a much older version of Niall. "I'm not really sure, sir."

"Well, if you're looking for a job, we could use a little help around here." He nodded toward the open door behind him. "I'll be out in the field, so I can't be here with Annie and she can't seem to run the computers to order supplies and the like." He stopped and waited.

Annie raised her clasped hands to her chest, hope filling her brown eyes. Joni's wolf may not be making her presence known by allowing her to shift, but Joni still felt her. Like now, when the two older people stood staring at her. "I'd like that very much. Do you need me to fill out some forms?"

Hollis tilted his head, making her think he appeared very wolf-like as he stared her down. A shiver wracked her frame, but she stood straighter. He inhaled deeply, then looked down at Annie who stared back at him. If she didn't know better, she'd swear they communicated in those few seconds before he looked back at her. "Annie will get you all set up. I got to get back to the fields and see to the boys. I'll make sure you both get home safe tonight. Where you staying...Vanessa?"

Joni bit her lip; blood filled her mouth before she licked it away. "I'll probably hit one of the hotels for the night, then look for something a little more permanent tomorrow or the next."

"Why don't you come home with me. We've got a small loft apartment that's clean and available. Plus, it's safer than anything you'll find in three counties."

Her wolf sat up inside Joni, warning bells going off. Why would these strangers be so nice to her? "Oh, that's too kind."

Hollis snorted. "It's not kind at all. Annie's lonely out on the farm now that I'm in the field and our boys are off, and she's all alone, sort of. Trust me, Vanessa, you'll be doing me a huge favor if you take the loft apartment. Hell, I should probably pay you." He laughed as he caught a pack of gum Annie tossed at him. "Think about it, and let Annie know. If you'd rather stay at one of the hotels, you've got several to choose from, but I'd recommend one of the mom and pop ones as they give a weekly rate that allows you access to laundry facilities and the like. Now, give me a kiss, woman, before I leave." Hollis tugged Annie toward him, turning so his back blocked Joni's view of them.

She looked around the interior of the gas station, liking how clean and organized it was compared to the others she'd seen. Her wolf gave a nudge of agreement, the first she'd truly gotten from the beast in a long time. Once Hollis walked out the door, she and Annie walked into the office where the computer was set up. Every couple of minutes, the bell would ring as a customer came in, but other than that, Joni and Annie worked to order items and got acquainted with each other. When it was closing time, Joni knew she'd be following Annie out to the farm. "Thank you for the job and the place to stay," Joni whispered. She waited as Annie locked the station up, looking around the darkness.

Annie patted her arm. "I know good when I see it, Vanessa. Come on, let's head home. I put a roast on with potatoes and carrots before I left his morning." Annie pulled her in for a quick hug. "I'm starving, how about you?" she asked, ignoring Joni's discomfort.

Joni's eyes watered at the ease the woman had with her affection. "Me too." In more ways than one, but she kept that to herself.

Atlas let out the breath he'd been holding when his sister finally walked out the door. The anger toward her mother was written on her face. Goddess, he hated that his entire family was being flipped upside down because of this bullshit. Things would change once he was alpha.

"You ready, Shauny?"

Shauny nodded. "How about you? Are you ready for what's coming?"

He snorted. "No, but I guess that don't matter. Let's do this."

A door inside the house slammed, making his sister jump. "You don't have to go with me," he assured her.

His sister bumped his arm with her own. "I'd walk over hot coals for any of my brothers. Going to the alpha house, a house that's soon to be yours? That's a walk in the park. Let's do this," she said with a laugh.

His two older brothers met them by the driveway, both dressed a little nicer than before, with flannel shirts that didn't have holes in them and jeans that were slightly less worn. Atlas raised his chin in acknowledgement, getting a similar chin raise from Atika and a middle finger from Abyle.

"Dear Goddess, save me from alpha males." Shauny stomped to the passenger seat of Atlas's vehicle, getting in before any of them could say a word or open her door.

"What did we do?" he asked.

Abyle shrugged, getting in behind Shauny followed by Atika. None of them looked back toward the house except Atlas, who glared toward the front window where their mother stood with her arms crossed. He gave her a two finger salute, then he too got inside. "Alright, kids, keep your fingers and toes inside the vehicle at all times. Insurance does not cover ignorance." He pushed the button, allowed the engine to purr for a second, before pushing his foot down on the gas spinning out of the driveway like the fires of hell were chasing them, just because he could.

The three squeals and growls coming from his siblings could be the last fun things he had to look forward to for a long time, and he'd be damned if he didn't take advantage of the times he had with them.

"I will smack the stupid right out of you, Atlas, you shithead," Atika promised.

Atlas looked at his older brother through the rearview mirror, laughing when he caught him holding onto the oh shit handle for dear life. Minutes later, he spotted the turnoff to the alpha's cabin and knew his good time was coming to an end. "Thanks for riding with me," he murmured.

"Yeah, well thanks for shoving my balls up to my throat," Abyle growled halfhearted.

"Now you can have one of the hussies kiss you and tell her she can lick your balls just by french kissing you," Shauny laughed.

Atika snorted. "That's so wrong on too many levels I can't even begin to explain, sister. Nope, I just can't. You ready, Atlas?"

Taking a deep breath, Atlas drove around the semi-circle, his eyes widening at the amount of vehicles that were there. "Why hadn't you guys been invited?"

"Probably because mom is a bitch. I bet they didn't think you'd come home first either." Shauny leaned between the seats and asked her twin brothers. "Who's limo is that?"

Atika looked at Abyle, both men shook their heads.

"Must be the female they want me to mate. Fuck, I hate this shit. Why isn't there another white bear?" Atlas leaned his head back and closed his eyes.

Atika gripped his shoulder. "You, like our father, were born a grizzly who happens to shift into the great white bear. There's only one in every clan, Atlas. Our father, he was fucked up before we were born. It was by the grace of the Goddess that he mated with our mother and the Goddess saw fit to create you. You're nothing like him, so stop thinking you are. Embrace who and what you are and take your rightful place, brother."

When his other brother placed his hand on his shoulder where Atika had squeezed, agreeing, Atlas finally began to believe. However, his bear hated the thought of mating with anyone but Joni. Before he could change his mind and sentence his entire family to death, he flung his door open. "Let's do this," he growled.

The entire walk to the big house, he stayed focused, not allowing his bear to sway him, until he came face-to-face with a quivering little girl.

"So good of you to finally come home, Atlas." Matilda, the mate of the old alpha spoke in a level tone, daring him.

His head whipped to the side, breaking contact with the tiny female in front of him. Surely she wasn't who they expected him to mate with. "I believe I was to be here at two o'clock on the dot and it is"—he looked at his watch, checking the time, even though he knew exactly what time it was down to the second "—straight up two pm."

His attitude seemed to fluster the female clan leader for a moment. "Yes, well I'm glad to see you're not only punctual but good at keeping your word. I see you brought guests."

Atlas was a firm believer that you should always begin as you meant to go on. Meaning, if you allowed someone to walk all over you once, you'd best believe they'd do it all the fucking time. He wasn't going to allow this woman, or anyone for that matter, to do that to him ever again. "I did not bring any guests. I brought my family to my home. Now, let's get a few things straight shall we? This is the alpha home. I'm alpha as of this moment, mated or not. You are the old alpha's mate, meaning you will have a home on the estate, but not in this home. Is that clear?" He looked around at the wide-eyed stares of those in attendance.

"Well I never..." she broke off as he held up his hand.

"I'm sure you haven't, and that's because you had some pussyass fuckers as alphas. Now, we're here because you gave your last order as the mate of the old alpha. Where is the female I'm to mate with?" he growled, hating her for what she'd done.

She straightened her spine, a small grin appeared. "I'd like to introduce you to Farren Kline of the Red River Clan and her father Adon."

The small female from before was pushed forward by a big barrel of a man with dark red hair. Her red hair matched his, making him think that was the reason for the name of their clan. Fuck she didn't look much older than fifteen years old. "What the fuck is the meaning of this?"

"What do you mean?" the big red haired man asked.

Atlas pointed at the quivering girl. "She's a baby for fuckssake."

Several clan members laughed, making the young girl sniff, which made Atlas feel like a fucking asshole. "I apologize, young Farren, but there's no way I can mate with a child."

Farren shook her head. "I'm not a child, sir. I'm almost seventeen winters."

His head jerked back. Who the hell talked like that, and where the fuck were they even from? "That's a child in my world, girl. In fact, it's illegal in I think every damn state." He crossed his arms over his chest, hoping the rest of his clan agreed.

The female he hated almost as much as his mother stepped forward. "We don't abide by human rules, Atlas, you know this. Her parents and clan have agreed to the mating, and I've accepted the pact. It is all but done. You must do your duty to your clan." She smirked.

Atlas narrowed his eyes, his senses picked up on the scent of fear wafting off the child who was slated to be his fucking mate. Over his dead fucking body. "I will not mate her until she has reached eighteen winters and only if I have not or if she has not found our truemates. If the Goddess sees fit to gift either of us such, then a mating set up will be put aside. This is my first law as alpha," he said, then turned away.

"You can't do that," she sputtered.

Atlas spun so fast, his chest nearly bumped into Matilda. "I can and I will. You are no longer in charge. I'll give you an hour to gather your things. As for you," his said softly, his eyes seeking the child they wanted him to mate. "Go home to your clan. On your eighteenth birthday, return unless you've found your truemate, or I've found mine." Goddess he was sure Joni was his. His bear was ready to rip out of him at the thought of the only female it wanted. If only he'd...no, he'd known it had been too soon to take that step with her. She'd been like an injured cub in need of care.

"No, we will stay here while the two of you get to know one another. That way when its time, you and my girl will have a mating like her mother and I."

Atlas wanted to claw the big red haired man's eyes out. Sanity kept him from moving forward, or rather his sister's hand on his arm did. "I don't believe I invited you, and as the alpha of White Bear Clan, it's my right to do so. I have a lot of things to learn and oversee. Taking on being a host to you, isn't on my itinerary."

"What my brother means is that there are many duties he's going to be seeing to, and although he'd love nothing better than to laze about and get to know your lovely daughter and your clan, he needs to focus on this clan. As an alpha yourself, I think you understand that duty to your clan comes first," Shauny said, sweetness coating her words.

"If I wasn't already mated to my sweet Farrah, I'd swear you were perfect for me. You are right, though. My Farren will be eighteen in a year and a half. That means in a year, we will be back, seeing as all the bears in my clan have already been tested as her truemate."

Atlas growled, stepping forward. "She's mated with every male in your clan? She's just a child," he spat.

Red fur spouted on Adon's face. "You do not speak of my daughter like that."

He got in the other man's face. "What the hell do you mean then?"

"I meant, I've had every male in my clan in her presence. If there was a truemate match, both of their bears would've known the other for who they were."

He took a deep breath, hoping for a calmness he didn't feel. No, he didn't want to mate the girl, but he'd be damned if he allowed any male, father or not, to willingly give a female to a line of men. "Explain," he gritted out between his teeth.

Adon looked at Atlas, then at the gathering around them. "Have none of you ever had a truemate bond?"

A couple of mated pairs stepped forward, the love between them clear. "Yes, I can see you know what I speak of." Adon nodded. "The rest of you just mate with another and accept that as fate?"

Matilda stepped forward. "You've signed a pact, giving your youngest daughter to our alpha. Is that not the same thing, if not worse?"

Atlas hated that she was right, yet he wasn't on board with the pact and knew it wouldn't be coming to fruition. In fact, he planned to hit the road once he solidified his place as alpha.

The other alpha's face turned a deeper shade of red. "My hope was they'd find love between one another. I was told he was a young alpha. Although he's younger than most, he's still not the twenty some I was led to believe," Adon said with a little less heat than before.

"I'm sure you were all expecting more than just me taking my place as alpha, but as you can see, there will be no mating today. So, let me formally state for all present. I, Atlas Braun of White Bear Clan am the alpha of the clan. Does anyone challenge me?" He felt the ripple flow over him at the announcement as if a mantle of power had been waiting on him to accept his place. The presence of his bear felt closer to the surface, yet Atlas didn't feel the need to rip things to shreds.

"I second him," Atika growled.

Abyle moved to stand on Atlas's other side. "I third them."

A rumble of approval rolled through the huge room.

"I guess that means nobody challenges my brothers." Shauny glared at Matilda. "Do you need help getting your stuff together, or have you already packed?"

"I'll need more than an hour to get all my things." Matilda looked around the great hall and all the glittering things.

"When my mate and I redecorate, we'll give you first dibs. Until then, you only take your personal things from your suite. You're down to fifty minutes," Atlas spoke low, letting Matilda hear the truth in his words. This woman was determined to manipulate him for reasons he still didn't know, but he'd be sure to find out. Until then, he wouldn't allow her to go too far from his sight.

"Shauny, why don't you help Matty with her packing?"

"My name is Matilda, and I don't need the help from one such as…I'll be fine on my own, thank you." Matilda turned on her heels, stomping through the crowd and up the grand staircase.

"You've made an enemy of that one, brother," Atika said, nodding toward the top of the stairs where they could see the older woman pause as she looked over her shoulder at them.

Abyle gave her a two finger wave, to which she gave a low growl they all could hear with their shifter hearing.

"My last fuck was given years ago, brother. By the way, thank you for standing with me tonight, all of you."

All three of his siblings blinked, then he was slapped on the back by his brothers with murmurs of no thanks needed before they slipped away into the crowd. His sister stood next to him a few minutes more before she finally rocked back on her heels. "So, what's her name?"

Chapter Three

Atlas shook his head, trying to ignore his sister and her question. "I need a drink."

"What you need is to answer my question and quit trying to evade them with alcohol. Besides, you know there's not enough liquor to get your big bear ass drunk." Shauny followed him through the crowd, yelling *move it* to those who were stupid enough to try and stop them.

"Shauny, you can't be rude to our clan. I'm alpha now, that makes you...something. Shit, what does that make you?"

"Pfft, it makes me the sister of the alpha. I was the daughter of the alpha. In this fucked up clan, it makes me shit. Now, stop changing the subject and tell me who she is." Shauny grabbed the bottle of beer from his hand, downing it before he could take a sip. "I can do this all night. I will be like a tick on a hound dog that's been on a hunting trip for way too long."

"Does that even make fucking sense to anyone?" Atlas looked at the ceiling, then back down at his little sister.

Abyle stood in the doorway. "Yeah, it means she's not letting it go until you tell her whatever it is she wants to know. I know from experience she's like a dog with a bone."

Atlas looked to where Abyle leaned against the doorframe as casual as you will, and then at his sister, her stance just as casual as she sat on top of the granite counter, her legs swinging back and forth, back and forth. "Her name is Joni."

Both of his siblings smiled, big, white toothy grins.

"Is she your truemate?" Atika asked.

He let out a sigh, then turned to see his other brother standing across the room. "How long you been there?"

"Long enough to see you squirming like a worm on the hook of a fishing pole."

"At least you didn't use another damn dog reference," Atlas sighed.

"So, when do we get to meet her? What clan is she from?" Shauny asked.

His stomach twisted at her questions. Atlas shook his head. "We'll talk about it after everyone leaves."

Abyle nodded, his head jerked as if he heard something. "I'm going to go check on the old lady of the house. I have a feeling she's going to be more trouble than we anticipated. Atika, keep an eye on these two."

Atlas felt a conversation flow between his twin brothers and wished, not for the first time he had their connection. "Can I have that beer now, sis?"

"I guess, you big baby. Try to keep your head on straight. I have a feeling we're gonna need all our focus in the coming months."

His bear seemed to nod inside him, making him swallow the drink down too quickly causing him to cough.

"Damn, baby bro, you need a sippy cup to drink out of?"

Atlas swiped out at Atika, barely missing his face with the monstrous claws his white bear sported, chuckling as his brother jumped back with a yelp. "I'll give you a sippy cup to drink out of, but not because you might spill, but because I've knocked all your teeth out."

"Vicious. I like it. Let's go see if the visiting clan have departed, then kick the other fuckers out. I'm tired from working in the fields. Tomorrow's going to be a long ass day."

For a moment, he looked his older brother over, noticing the slight changes in both Atika and Abyle. They were only a couple years older, but they'd been made to work the farm and be the men of the house since they were teens, whereas Atlas was made to learn all about becoming an alpha and leader.

"Don't look at us with pity, boy. Our lives are our own. At any time, we could've left and found a clan to join, or gone rogue. We stayed because we believed in you. Don't make us regret our choices." Atika grabbed Atlas by the shoulders, gave him a small shake, then pounded his back. "You grew up big and right. We can see you, truly see you. One day, we'll explain, but for now, let's go shove some freeloaders out."

The true joy in his older brother's tone had Atlas smiling. "Try not to shove too hard."

"I can't make that promise. I mean, if I stumble and they are right...there. Woops." He grinned, showing white teeth with a couple that were longer than the others. Yeah, his bear was close to the surface.

Joni looked around at the small yet cozy little apartment above the barn that Annie had shown her to. It had an open floor plan with the bedroom and bathroom being the exception, but she loved it. "Goddess, it's perfect, Annie. So light and airy even though it's small. How'd you do all this up here?"

She bit her lip, hoping the older woman didn't think she was putting her down.

"Ah, it was easy really. You see, we have all kinds of help around here. I told Hollis this was wasted space, and that our kids might want a place to escape when they came home. So one day, he and a few of our boys decided to make it happen."

"What she's not telling you is that she twisted my arm, and the boys' too, until we did," Hollis said with a smile in his tone.

Joni kept from jumping, barely.

"Girl, what I gotta do, wear a bell around my neck?" Hollis asked with a grin. "I swear I smelled that roast a mile away. Come on woman, feed me. I mean, look at me. My stomach is darn near eating my backbone." Hollis patted his stomach, which was flat, yet he was nowhere near skinny.

Annie snorted. "This man is always starving, Vanessa. Come on, let's go eat, then you can come back and settle in."

Joni couldn't find a way to politely decline and honestly didn't want to. Heck, the scent of roast could be smelled from the open windows, making her stomach growl loud enough even the two older people, who weren't shifters had to be able to hear it. "That sounds lovely, Annie. Thank you for—well, thank you for everything you've done for me today." Her cheeks heated at her words.

Annie took her hand. "Nonsense, child. You came along at the right time to the right place. Or is it the right place at the right time. Whatever it is, I needed help and so did you. It's a win win for the both of us. Now, let's go eat before Hollis decides to gobble it all," Annie whispered loudly.

"I heard that," Hollis called back up the stairs.

Joni couldn't contain the smile at their banter. One day if she were blessed to find a mate, she hoped they loved like the Wilde's.

The big house was similar to the barn loft but filled with much more...love and things. Good goddess, she lost count as she looked at all pictures Annie had had taken of the boys and girls, she'd claimed as her own throughout the years. "Are you like official foster parents, or what?"

Hollis paused with a fork full of mashed potatoes and a huge piece of roast near his lips. "Not quite as formal as that. We are more like magnets for lost boys and girls, or young men and women like yourself. I don't know how to explain it, but," he trailed off, shrugged then took his bite of food, the discussion seemingly over.

Joni looked at Annie, who nodded, her fork scraping up the last of the gravy on her plate, with a sweet smile on her face.

"What happens to them, you know, after?" Joni couldn't let it go.

Hollis sighed, setting his fork down on the empty plate. "What do you mean after?"

She was surprised to find her own plate only had a few pieces of corn left on it and was loathed to leave them uneaten. Before answering, she stabbed with the end of her tines, placing them in her mouth, enjoying the sweet flavor before answering. "I mean, where do they go after they leave here?" Gah, now that the question was asked, it sounded stupid. If they were serial killers, they weren't going to just spout it out. Besides, she was a wolf, even if her stupid beast wouldn't exactly come out.

"Most are still here, working the farm or in town. Is this your way of asking if we have nefarious intentions, Vanessa?" Hollis asked bluntly, his eyes holding hers.

It took everything in her to not look away. "Yes," she agreed.

"Good girl, although if we were, we probably wouldn't have told you the truth. However, my Annie is an angel straight to the core of her. Now me, I'm only good because of her. I swear to you as long as my girl is on this Earth, I'll be as good as she is." Hollis placed his hand over Annie's.

"See what he does to me. This man right here has the ability to make this old woman tear up and ruin her makeup." Annie wiped her hand beneath her eyes.

Joni felt a pang in her chest, wishing she'd find the same thing, knowing her chance had left with a stubborn bear didn't help. "I'm sorry," she whispered.

Annie reached across the table, joining the three of them. "Never apologize for thinking of your own safety. Now, who wants pie?"

"I don't think I could fit another thing inside me," Joni swore.

"I told you my girl was the best cook." Hollis grabbed Annie when she stood up, stopping her when she reached for his plate.

"Oh, I agree, Hollis. Annie is the best cook in all of Texas. Heck, maybe all of America." Joni sat back, patting her stomach.

Hollis patted his face with his napkin. "Trust me, you really do want to save room for this dessert."

Joni groaned. "Seriously, where do you put it?" She looked at Hollis's and Annie's slim but fit figures.

Annie walked in, the sweet scent of banana hitting Joni and had her leaning forward. "Is that banana cream pie? Like homemade banana cream pie?"

"My girl is famous for her pies, but this one she saves for me and contests. Let me tell you, it's rare that I share." Hollis's eyes twinkled.

Joni licked her lips. "I'm prepared for a food coma just for a slice of that pie."

"Um, a food coma?" Annie asked.

"I think she means she'd like a slice." Hollis pulled the pie in front of him, taking the knife and cutting a huge piece for himself. "Do you want a piece this size or smaller?"

"Holy crap. If I eat a piece that big, I'll need you to roll me up the stairs." Joni laughed.

Hollis waited until he heard Joni's soft even breathing before he turned to his mate of over seventy years. "She's a wolf," he murmured.

Annie nodded. "I know, but I can barely scent her animal."

He pulled her back into his chest, both staring toward the barn from the back porch. They'd taken over running the pack of misfits, or as he liked to call them, the lost, over sixty years ago by happenstance. They too had been lost themselves, running from packs who wouldn't accept them as a mated pair even though they were fated to be there by the Goddess herself. "What do you think happened to her?"

Annie tilted her head to the side, her glorious hair still in a loose bun on top, tickling his nose. "Whatever it is, we need to fix it."

"You always want to fix them, my girl," he chuckled, nuzzling her neck where his mark was.

She shivered, her little body rubbing against his. "Of course I do. It's what we do."

Hollis nodded, knowing there was nothing else to say. "We let her come to us though. I scented a deep sadness and the beginnings of a mating on her. If she's running from a mate, I don't want to interfere just yet. Or if this is a set up, I won't allow our family to be hurt." He didn't try to suppress his beast as he said those words.

Annie turned in his arms, her blue eyes sparkling. "I'd never ask you to. Our children come first, last, and middle, always."

A snort escaped him. "Those children are grown men and women who could wipe the Earth with most who come trying to fuck with them, girl," he rumbled.

She swatted his arm. "They'll always be my children."

He bent his head, his lips sweeping across hers. "That's why I love you and will always love you, my sweet girl."

Her lips opened beneath his like he knew they would, just like they'd done all these years. Just as they'd done that first time those many moons ago, and like he knew they'd do each and every time for as long as the Goddess blessed them. "Thank you for loving me, Annie," he whispered.

"Shut up and make love to me, Hollis Wilde." She stood on her tip toes, opening her mouth for his tongue, her arms tightening around his shoulders, her legs lifting around his waist while his arms secured her to him.

"I love it when you get bossy," he bit out between kisses, turning back toward the open door to the house. His ears listened to the wind, catching distant conversation while his senses checked for any disturbance that shouldn't be. Finally, when he knew all was well, he kicked the door shut and walked his mate back to their bedroom, making love to her for hours. He howled, letting the others know they were on duty, getting several answering calls back.

Joni heard howling rent the air. Not knowing what kind of animals made those kinds of noises had her heart nearly crashing through her chest. She sat up against the iron headboard clutching the sheet between her fists. Her wolf raked against her skin yet wouldn't come out. "You scaredy puppy," she whispered in the dark. Her eyes adjusted, making out the shapes of the room. With a quick glance at her watch, she realized it was just past three thirty in the morning, almost two and a half hours before she was due to meet with Annie and open the store. "Well, at least I can see in the dark, so there's that," she muttered.

Being a shifter who couldn't shift anymore sucked hairy monkey balls. Her thought made her giggle. Someone had to of sucked a monkey ball in order to realize it wasn't a good thing, or they had a really good imagination. She hoped it was the latter instead of the former. Deciding her sleep for the night was done, she got out of bed. Without turning on any lights, since she didn't want to wake the Wilde's, she fixed the covers, placing the decorative pillows back how Annie had them. The kitchen had a Keurig, which she quickly turned on, then she took a quick shower. By the time she got out, the coffee machine was ready for a quick cup and so was she. Joni wasn't quite a bear without coffee, but she definitely needed a pick me up after only five hours of sleep.

Her watch read four fifteen, leaving her a lot of time left to sit and do nothing, or she could go for a run. Hollis and Annie didn't say she was to stay inside, and it wasn't as if she was going to go far. Since her wolf was being a riotous brat, Annie needed to burn energy and found running a great way to do it.

With her running shoes on along with the proper clothing, she set out, finding a trail that looked like it was regularly used. She plopped her earbuds in and ran, her legs and arms moving while she let her mind wander. Her wolf, while unable to burst free, moved closer to the surface, making Joni sigh with contentment. Out here on the farm, she could run faster, allowing herself more freedom to be more like herself and not worry human eyes could see she wasn't quite like them.

She was so lost in her thoughts and the ease it was to move along the well beaten path, she didn't notice that anyone was trailing her until she nearly ran into the chest of the huge man. A gasp escaped her, followed by a scream that had birds taking flight.

Joni pulled an earbud out. "Holy shit! I'm sorry. I didn't see you there," she breathed out, taking a step backward. Fuck, he was huge, and menacing looking, wearing only a pair of low slung sweatpants with sweat rolling down his chest.

"You should watch where you're going, little one. There's danger all around you," he growled.

She nodded, looking around and noticing she couldn't see the farm or anything familiar. Of course, she only had to turn around and run back the way she'd come, her mind and body had a way of zeroing in on things like that. However, if this big behemoth of a man decided to pounce, she'd be screwed. *Gah, don't think like that Joni.*

"Where you coming from?" he asked.

Joni waved her hand behind her. "I'm staying with the Wilde's," she answered honestly.

The man's shoulders relaxed; a sigh escaped. "Another lost one, huh? Let me show you the way back." He waved a hand toward the trail.

She shook her head. "I can find my way, thank you," she argued.

He took a deep breath, then let it out. "What are you?"

"What do you mean?"

"Ah, there you are. Annie was worried when she called on you for breakfast. You an early morning runner, Vanessa?"

Joni spun to face Hollis. "Son-of-a-bitch, Hollis, you're gonna give me a heart attack." Her hand went to her chest. "You know this guy?" She pointed with her thumb over her shoulder toward the shirtless man.

Hollis nodded. "Yep, that's Oaklyn. He's one of ours."

"Do all your people walk around half nekkid?" She looked Oaklyn up and down, taking in the fact he wore nothing but a pair of sweats.

Oaklyn shrugged. "My cabin's over there. I heard you running out here and came to see who it was. I only had time to slip something on, otherwise you'd have had a real eyeful." He winked.

"Oak," Hollis warned.

The big man named Oaklyn or Oak just grinned. "Since she appears to be harmless, I'm heading back to get ready for the day. She going to be around long?"

"We'll see," Hollis said.

Joni was sure she heard a growl, almost as if he was warning the other man, but then again her stomach was rumbling something fierce. Obviously last night's feast had made her appetite grow, and now she'd need to eat more, which meant she'd need to work out more since she wasn't shifting and expending the energy like most shifters. Or, she'd become even curvier.

"Come on, I'll walk back with you." Hollis held his arm out.

"Oh, you came looking for me? I'm sorry. I didn't mean to worry you two. I usually go for a run in the mornings. I should've told you guys." She ducked her head.

Hollis touched her ear, the earring covered most of the damage. "This had to have hurt," he stated, his voice deep and angry.

"It happened a long time ago." Her hand came up, covering the damage.

"Annie made waffles. I hope you like them." His gruff change of subject didn't go unnoticed, nor did she miss the words he muttered too low for most humans to hear of him calling her a liar, but there was no heat behind them. No, she only felt compassion rolling off him.

"I love waffles, but my ass and hips are probably going to hate them." She grinned.

Chapter Four

Joni added another item to the spreadsheet shaking her head at the jumbled mess Annie had the books in. Lordy the woman had no clue how to keep the items properly placed in order to know what she's sold, compared to what hadn't. How she's kept her taxes was anyone's guess, but obviously it had worked, however Joni was going to make it easier for the older woman if she had to drag Annie kicking and screaming into the computer age. An image of her doing just that had her snorting. Annie may be older, but she looked like she could wipe the ground with Joni's carcass and still take on some others. Her sense of hearing let her know she was no longer alone in the small office, making her look up to see a smiling Annie. "Alright, I've got you set up with all your stock right here." She pointed at the computer monitor. "All you'll need to do is come in here each week and add in when you get a shipment. However, before adding, let's just go out and count how many you currently have, delete it from the stock and then," Joni paused at Annie's wide eyed look. "What's the matter?"

Annie smiled. "You make it sound so easy."

"It is easy. If you get a new item, you just add it here." Joni showed her how, even going so far as to create a small notebook for Annie. "Just in case I'm not here when it happens."

"You're a good girl, Vanessa." Annie wrapped her arms around Joni, squeezing her hard.

"Nah, I'm a good worker. Now, let's go out with this here and take real stock." Joni tapped the papers she had clipped to the clipboard, then handed another to Annie, laughing at the other woman's groan.

"I take it back. You're a...you're a beastly taskmaster." Annie took her clipboard, and the two of them went to work, counting items that were on their lists, each taking turns when a customer came in to ring them up.

Joni paused when Annie stood up, a low growl coming from the other woman. "I hate that man with every fiber of my being." Annie spat.

The man in question was walking toward them dressed in a suit that Joni knew had to cost way more than she'd spent on her entire wardrobe. "Who is he?"

Annie waved her hand as the door opened. "Afternoon Mikey, what brings you in today?"

"It's Michael now, Annabel. Where's your..." he paused as he noticed Joni. "Ah, who do we have here, another lost one you're trying to save?"

The older woman stepped in front of Joni. "That's none of your concern. I don't believe we have anything you want here, Mikey."

Joni thought it strange the way the newcomer spoke, and the way Annie tried to protect her, but the other man gave her the creeps. Although she wanted to run to the office and hide, she didn't want to leave Annie alone to face the other man. He reminded her of Keith in a slimy, I'm all up in my own ass kind of way.

"Ah, there's Hollis now. Did you want to speak with him?" Joni asked.

Mike the douchenozzle froze, his assuredness not quite so apparent. "No, I stopped by to see if you were ready to sell this place yet?"

Annie rolled her eyes. "My answer is the same as always. No."

"One day your answer will be yes to all my questions."

"Her answer will always be no, Mikey. Now, unless you want my fist to meet your face again, I suggest you take yourself and your fancy suit out of my space." Hollis cracked his neck back and forth. The flannel shirt he wore, stretched at the seams and was only partially buttoned, while the jeans he wore looked like they'd seen better days.

"Still uncivilized I see, Hollis," Mike sneered.

Hollis looked Mikey up and down. "Still a pussy in a suit I see, Mikey. You want to tangle with me, again?"

Mike took a step backward, followed by another until he reached the door. Joni could smell fear and power. Goodness, Hollis was letting off so much power she'd swear he was an alpha in human skin.

"One day, you'll get knocked down, and I'll be there to watch it," Michael promised, took one last look over his shoulder before walking out the door. The car he got into looked too small for a man of his size, but he folded himself in and roared off.

Joni raised her hand before speaking. "Okay, first of all let me say, wow. Second, did you see that roller skate on wheels he got into. How the fuck did he fold himself into it?"

Hollis looked at her then Annie, then burst into laughter. "Kid, I've asked myself that many times and still have no damn clue. I think he has no balls, which means he can bend himself into a pretzel. You two okay?"

Annie walked up to him and buried her face into his chest, her arms wrapping around him. "I hate him so much."

Hollis rubbed his cheek over the top of her head. "I know, baby. Vanessa, can you hold down the fort here for a few while me and Annie go into the office?"

Joni lifted her clipboard. "No problem. You two take your time." She heard a slight sniff and hated Mikey for making Annie cry, but loved Hollis for being there to make her better. As soon as the door shut, her mind raced, wondering how the other man knew to come running. A look at the clock showed it was almost lunch time, so she brushed it off that'd he'd been planning to come for lunch. "Oh shit, was he coming for a nooner?" she whispered as she looked at the closed office door, but she didn't hear anything. Although her wolf was suppressing itself, she still had excellent hearing. Not wanting to overhear them, she popped her earbuds in and went to work taking down stock.

Atlas ran a tired hand over his face, the taillights of the last vehicle disappearing down the lane. Oh, he had no delusions there would be some grumblings come morning light, but they'd meet with the same answer he gave tonight, which was a big fat fuck you. He was the destined white bear, or so says the prophecy. The only shocking thing from the evening was that his mother hadn't shown her face, especially with all her children there. Hell, he'd almost been prepared to be—cordial in the eyes of the clan. Thankfully he hadn't had to.

"Mother is probably making plans on how and when to show up with demands. Ya know, being she's the matriarch and all," Shauny snarled, plopping down on the sofa nearest the window.

He looked over his shoulder, taking in her tired appearance. "You staying the night?"

Shauny kicked one leg over the arm negligently while she bit on her thumbnail, her eyes glassy. "Does this place bring back any memories for you?" she asked.

Abyle walked in, coming to a hard stop at her question. "Memories? Yeah, I remember having to cut my own switch from the backyard so that bastard could strap me for whatever reason he felt I'd fucked up. Did you know if you remove all the leaves from one of them suckers, and a man with the kind of strength dear old dad had, a single strike can almost slice straight to the bone?" he asked almost casually.

"Don't," Atika snarled. "She's not to blame for the sins of the father."

"Fuck, Shauny, I'm sorry." Abyle lumbered over to the sofa, sitting next to their shocked sister, his arm sweeping her into his side. "Daddy dearest was a mean bastard on the best days, at the end."

Atlas turned back toward the window. He'd known their dad had whipped both twins, hell, he himself had experienced a strapping more than a few dozen times, had the scars to prove it. Unlike his brothers, he hadn't gotten his marks covered with tattoos. As the white bear, it had been physically beaten into him not to mar his skin, or the Goddess wouldn't bless him with the gifts needed for the future. Now, looking out at the darkness, he thought of Joni and wished things were different. Wished for things to be different. Only a look backward and the words he'd heard from the ethereal female they worshipped reminded him there were things greater than his own needs. His heart ached, the painful loss of his truemate nearly brought him to his knees. Now that he'd taken the mantle of alpha, he could follow his heart, doing exactly what the Goddess had planned.

"Atlas, did you hear me?" Shauny asked, touching his arm.

He took a deep breath, closing his eyes. "Sorry, can you repeat that, I was thinking of a million things." Not a total lie.

"We came with you, so unless you're going to take us home, you gonna let me borrow your vehicle?" She blinked innocently up at him.

He heard a loud cough from behind her, glancing up to see Abyle shaking his head, his hands around his throat dramatically. "Err, how about I drive you back? I could use some fresh air anyhow."

Shauny looked over her shoulder, then back at him with a glare. "Which one of those asshats did it?"

Atlas tried to act innocent, but a smile split his lips. "No clue what you're talking about. So, you ready?" He pulled his keys out, tossing them in the air, catching them before she could, knowing he was teasing her, something he'd missed doing.

"Oh, I see how it is. You three going to stick together then? Fine, but remember, I always get even, and when I do, you'll be begging me for mercy." She turned and flipped her hair over her shoulder with a huff, heading toward the huge entryway door.

"Ah shit, you two done pissed baby bear off," Atika joked.

Their sister raised her right hand in the air, middle finger extended. "Sit and spin, asswipes, but just remember this when you need me to intervene on your behalf."

Abyle shrugged. "Guess we'll just have to be more—inventive ourselves."

"You mean you'll have to stop inviting every bitch in heat at the local bars to come back to your place, then when they want to stay the night, you call up sis here to come and tell them party is over in a sweet way?"

"Yep, now I'll just tell them they can come back with me for a good time, but when we're done, they gotta go. If they ain't on board with it, then bye Felicia." Abyle waved his hand at the end.

Atlas looked to the ceiling, then at his twin brothers. "Does he really get laid with that attitude?"

Atika lifted his right shoulder. "I think it's 'cause he looks like me."

"Oh my gawd, you two are too much. Please, take me home before their heads inflate so much they won't be able to fit in a vehicle. Oh wait, that might be good, then they'd have to shift and run home," she said with glee.

In that very moment, he remembered why he'd die for the three people in the room with him. They were his family. Until Joni, they were the only people on Earth who mattered more than his own life. "Alright you three, party's over, let's get you home before you turn into mice or some shit."

"Pretty sure that's not how the fairytale goes." Shauny linked her arm through his as they walked out the door. "You gonna lock that?"

He thought of all who could get in whether it was locked or not. "Nah, if someone wants in that badly, they'll get in."

His brothers stopped walking, turning back toward him. With the moon overhead, they were illuminated, looking almost as if they were in a spotlight. "We'll be back after we grab a few things. You'll need to call a clan meeting tomorrow and begin putting those you trust in places of power. You don't have to put either of us in any certain place, but we will make sure you're protected." Abyle turned after his announcement, climbed into the back passenger seat, and slammed the door like he'd just told them the weather report.

"I second what he said," Atika agreed, his eyes fierce. "Anyone tries to hurt you; they'll have to go through the both of us first."

Shauny sniffed. "They love you. They really love you," she deadpanned.

"Did you just misquote Sally Fields?" Atlas asked as he held open the door for Shauny.

"I believe it was she who was misquoted in the first place, so whatevs. Home, James," she laughed, buckling into the seat while Atlas stared down at her.

"You really are a strange female." He was still smiling when he got behind the steering wheel. "Is Sonya going to give you a hard time?"

His question brought silence inside the SUV.

The lane to where his family lived loomed and still nobody spoke. His bear stirred, sensing danger. He pushed down on the brakes. "Anyone else feel something's off?"

Atika rolled his window down, the smell of fire hitting them all. "Fuck! Go, Atlas," he roared.

He'd already began driving, the SUV eating up the distance down the bumpy drive, smoke billowing up from the main house. Shauny cried out, her hand flying to the door handle. "Mama," she cried.

Atlas had cut off his connection to the woman, severed the familial tie, so whatever Shauny and his brothers felt didn't affect him, but their pain hit him like a fist to the heart.

He'd pulled to a rocking stop seconds before his three siblings leapt out their doors, shifting into their bears, running for the burning house. Atlas realizing what they'd planned, quickly followed, his white grizzly twice as big as any of their animals, and three times as powerful, landed with a thud in front of theirs, roaring a warning, his alpha power halting their movements.

"Stop. I sense no heartbeat inside there. She's gone. I order you three to stand down, now," he ordered through their link.

Atika shifted first, sweat, anger, and sadness poured off his naked form. "Motherfucker, don't alpha order me from saving my mother," he roared almost as loudly as Atlas, but he didn't disobey.

Abyle staggered to his knees after shifting. "What the hell?" He shook his head.

Shauny was the last to shift, sobs making her words incoherent. "Why? Why did you stop us? I know you hate her, but she's our mother. I'll never forgive you, Atlas," she cried.

Atlas roared, her words making his white bear angrier than he'd ever been. The mantle of alpha being forced on him, the power he'd been given, his first duty to save his brothers and sister, appearing like a...like a fucking betrayal. Fuck that.

Shifting faster than he'd ever done, he let them see what he looked like beneath the clothes, allowed them to see the scars he possessed. They thought he got off easy, since he was younger than them. They were fucking wrong. The day he'd killed their father was because the bastard had decided he'd kill Atlas after overhearing the Goddess speak to him. Only Atticus wasn't content to do it the easy way. Oh no, he'd tried to eviscerate him first, offering up his entrails to the gods in exchange for power.

Shauny gasped. "What happened to you?" Her shaking hand reached for Atlas's chest, the thick scar bisecting his abs hard to miss. He couldn't count the number of white scars that striped across his chest, stomach, and lower. There literally wasn't an inch of his front or back that hadn't been laid open by a switch thanks to his father, many times while his mother watched, and even cheered. There had been something wrong with the both of them. They'd hated him yet loved all three of his siblings. He'd had to hide his injuries growing up, pretend all was fine, or else they'd do worse the next time. They'd even threatened to harm his siblings if he'd told anyone else, so he'd taken the beatings, the lashings without telling anyone.

"You want to know what happened to me? First of all, I saved all three of you just now. Open your senses. Do you hear her heart, or sense her? She's not in there. Hell, she's nowhere around here. Now, if you really want to know what happened to me, you better make for damn sure you really want the truth, because once you know, there's no going back." Atlas paced back and forth like a caged bear. His bear hadn't been out long enough, the need to roam, to reclaim their land, ate at them both.

Abyle moved in closer yet stayed far enough away he wouldn't be in danger of getting swiped with Atlas's claws. "Tell us," he said softly.

Atlas smiled, his alpha powers flowing through him. He knew his eyes were turning the light blue of his white bear, could see the fear in his siblings' eyes. "No, I think I'll show you instead." He opened his mind, linking with the three of them, taking them back to the last day he'd been with their dad.

26 years ago...

Atlas shook as he followed his father through the woods. He was only seven, but he knew his father didn't just take him on a hunting trip alone without a good reason, or more aptly, a terrible one. He rubbed his shoulder, feeling the healing scabs from the last lashing he'd gotten because he'd shifted faster than his father. Next time, he'd go slower.

The sound of water rushing had excitement stirring. Atlas loved to swim. When he was in the water, he could go all the way to the bottom and pretend for a little while he was a fish, and sometimes when he came back up, his father was nowhere to be seen.

"Did you hear me, boy, or you off in lalastupidland again? I told your mother you were touched in the head, but she didn't listen. Fucking Goddess, why she gifted you I'll never know, but I'm putting an end to it today, just like the gods did."

Atlas tried to pay attention to what he was saying but didn't know what he meant. How was he going to end things? He'd learned it was best to stay quiet.

"See, you're not special. If you were actually Goddess touched, you'd know what was coming." Atticus chuckled, tossed a leather bag down, and pulled out some rope followed by other supplies.

"Are we fishing?" he asked

Angry eyes glared at him. "Oh, I'll be fishing with the best bait, after. Now get your ass over here and help me put these in the ground."

Wanting to make his father happy, Atlas moved to do as he was told, picking up a metal looking poll with a spike in the end. Atticus began pounding one into the ground, telling Atlas where to put the one he held. Within minutes they had all four in the ground. "Now what?" he asked his father.

"Now you lay down in the middle of them."

A sliver of fear worked its way through him. "Wh...why?" he stammered.

"Because I told you to." Atticus backhanded Atlas, splitting his lip.

Within seconds, Atlas found himself tied to the stakes, his smaller bear no match to his father's. Through the woods he saw two sets of eyes staring back at him. His mother's brown accusing eyes were cold as always, and the head enforcer of the clan stood next to her. "Help me, mama. Please, don't let him do this."

Atticus stood above him with a wicked looking knife in his hand. "The way to end this supposed prophecy is to end you like the Gods did in times gone by." He brought the knife down, slicing through Atlas's stomach, searing pain making him scream.

A white light flashed, his bear roared, bursting out of him, and then darkness followed by the smell of blood, so much blood.

"Stop, Atlas, stop," Shauny begged.

"Goddammit, stop, brother." Atika fell to his knees, his nose bleeding.

Abyle held Shauny, tears rolling down their faces.

Atlas spun, shifting into his huge white bear, roaring up at the skies. *I'm sorry,* he said through their link. Then he severed their tie to him, not wanting them to feel his pain, hating himself for allowing them to see and feel the pain he'd felt that day all those years ago.

With his senses open, he heard the three of them say *I'm sorry* echo through the woods, but he couldn't allow himself to accept their apologies. He was the one who was sorry. He was the one who'd forced them to see and feel something they never should've experienced. It was he who was sorry. Goddess touched, his ass. He was the worst alpha ever.

His bear raced through the woods, running as if the hounds of hell were on his heels until he found himself in the same clearing as the one where he'd claimed his father's life, the same clearing he'd become not just a white bear, but a dire white bear. He wondered if his brothers and sister realized what they'd seen when he shifted, or if they put it down to his alpha bear. Either way, he wasn't just some white fucking bear that was prophesized to be an alpha.

No, on the day his father tried to kill him, he'd woken a beast inside a seven year old boy. A beast that relished in killing his father and then the enforcer. Atlas remembered standing over his mother, blood dripping from his fangs and nearly every inch of his huge bear, low growls emanating from him. He'd spoken to Sonya, only it had been a different being and him merging, making a pact with her. She agreed to raise his brothers and sister with love, as for him, he'd not asked for anything because it was clear he could take care of himself. She'd agreed to do so from that day until he became alpha. As the memory flashed, he realized she'd done as she'd agreed. Now that he was alpha, her reason to stay was gone, but she clearly wanted to send him a message with the burning of the house. Atlas shifted, sitting on a huge rock near the water's edge. "Had she ever loved any of her children?"

"I don't believe it's in her capacity to love anyone, or anything, other than herself."

Atlas spun, his claws out.

"Put those away," the Goddess said with ease.

He knew she could will him dead with a thought. In a moment, he was clothed in a pair of slacks and a button down shirt, both favorites from his closet. "This is something all of you can do with a thought. Something you've always had the ability but hadn't learned, a fault of mine." She waved her hand toward the rock he had been sitting on. "Please sit."

"Are you here to kill me?" He licked his lips, thinking of the last time he'd seen Joni, wishing he'd claimed her, then mentally smacked himself. At least this way, she wouldn't suffer the loss of a truemate.

The Goddess sighed. "Silly bear, of course I'm not here to kill you. However, you've been a very naughty bear. I had to fix your brothers and sister a little. Their pain called to me. You can't do what you did without repercussions. Showing them what that evil bastard did isn't something anyone, let alone someone who loves you, should see without warning. That is something no child nor adult should ever face."

Atlas jumped to his feet. "Their pain called to you? Their pain? How about my pain as a child? All the times they beat me? Was I not hurting enough for you? What? Did it take my father ripping my intestines out in order for you to notice me?" he roared, ripping his shirt open to show her the scars.

The Goddess floated forward, her hand touching his cheek. "After I came to you as a small child, I assumed you were protected and loved by your family. Never did I think one of my chosen, such as your father, could do what he—did. I'm sorry I wasn't there sooner. So sorry I didn't stop them sooner. Sorry, for failing you." A silver tear fell from her silver eyes.

Warmth flowed from her to him, healing the cracks around his heart, the scar on his chest, the one that always seemed to itch, all these years later from his father's favorite hunting knife, warmed. Atlas looked down, seeing the ugly jagged scar turn pink, then right before his eyes, the wound began to fade, then it was gone. "If I could I'd erase all the times from your memory, but to do that would change who you are, who you're meant to become. You see, I can take away your scars, but if I change one thing about the past, then your future, your now, changes. Would you want me to do that? Would you risk not knowing your Joni?" A silver glow emanated from her, encompassing him and her.

"No," he whispered.

The Goddess nodded. "You are who you are because of your past, not because of your scars. See, they're gone, but you're still you. Do you feel different?" She touched his chest.

Atlas put his hand where hers had touched. "No, and yes. I don't want you to change my past. Fuck, shit. I didn't...damn, I'm messing this up." He paced away, then came back. "I'm always running away. I'm done running. You gifted me with this." He pounded his chest. "My bear's not a beast; he's one of the best parts of me. That bastard who tried to kill me didn't give me a gift; you did." He nodded but didn't wait for her to speak. "I'm sorry I yelled at you, sorry I—cussed and...shit. I'm sorry for everything. Are my family okay?"

She lifted a hand. "They're coming through the clearing now. You can ask them yourself. Remember, with power comes great responsibility, Atlas. I know you think what you had to do all those years ago was awful, but you did what you had to do to survive. If you had to do it again today, would you?"

He didn't have to think just nodded. "If they'd succeeded in killing me, who's to say it wouldn't have been one of them next?"

Her palm pressed against his chest again. "And that's why you're a good alpha, my white bear. Your future isn't going to be easy, but it's going to be good if you follow your heart. Blessed be, Atlas."

His palm covered his racing heart, his mouth moving, saying the same words back to her. In a burst of color, the Goddess was gone, leaving him alone with the twins and Shauny.

"Please tell me I wasn't seeing things, and that was really a glowing female?" Atika asked.

"Oh my gawd, that was the Goddess, wasn't it?" Shauny asked, wonder filling her voice.

Atlas turned to face them, his shirt open, showing a smooth chest. "That was the Goddess," he agreed.

"I think she visited us after you did. The memory is fuzzy, but I have bits of pieces that I wish I didn't." Abyle put his hands in his pockets, his brown eyes looking anywhere but at Atlas.

"You can hate me if you want," he growled. Hell, he hated himself, had since he'd woke covered in his father's blood along with Dale's, the enforcer of the pack's.

"Hate you? You think we hate you? All we knew was that he'd had an accident while you and he were out hunting. Fucking hunting, something we'd never been allowed to do with our father. We were older, yet we'd never been asked to go, and we were so fucking jealous. We thought if we'd been there we could've saved him from dying. Now, we find out that he tried, nearly succeeded in ripping your guts out, only to die at the claws and fangs of your bear. Fuck, we owe you an apology, fealty, and our fucking lives." Abyle pounded his right fist on his chest. "I will have your back always. I'll place your life, the life of your cubs, above my own for the rest of my life," he promised, dropping to one knee.

Atika followed suit with Shauny coming to stand in front of him. "You're our brother; we love you. I'm sorry you suffered, but I'm glad the Goddess did whatever she did to our memories." She rubbed her temple. "I still feel residues of your pain, I just don't remember all of it, but I have a memory that will haunt me for always, only it was your memory. You have my fealty as well, for always." She dropped to one knee.

"Get up, all of you. You will never put your lives above mine, do you hear me?"

His siblings got up, smiling. "You ain't the boss of us, brother. Besides, I like you without the scar reminding us a whole lot better. Now, let's head back to your alpha house. Looks like I'm gonna need to go shopping tomorrow, so you're gonna need to access some funds." Shauny rubbed her hands together, clearly happy to change the subject.

Atlas and his brothers groaned. He opened his senses, sighing when he didn't feel any lingering anger between them. He sent a thank you out to the Goddess, knowing she'd helped with her healing powers. "I'm sorry for what I did before," he muttered.

His sister linked her arm through his. "You'll make it up to me tomorrow when you hear cha-ching, cha-ching, over and over again," she teased.

"I don't think she's joking. Our mother had her on a pretty tight budget when it came to buying anything." Atika said, his words sobering them all.

Chapter Five

The following morning came, making Atlas groan at the amount of stuff his sister amassed during their shopping trip into town. Not that she'd only bought for herself, but she'd also bought things for the alpha house she'd insisted he needed. "I don't think I have a need for all that," he muttered.

"Of course, you do. Every alpha needs to have his own towels. You don't want to wash your ass with the same towels the old bitch and her people have, or your face with ones that touched their asses?" She pretended to wipe her butt, then put it to her face.

Put that way, Atlas agreed. Hell, the way his sister put everything, he'd agreed. Several hours later, he was thinking they'd need a rental trailer to haul their purchases home, but the joy in Shauny's features kept him from making a snarky response. "Dinner?" he asked their group, his stomach growling loudly enough the girl behind the counter grinned.

"What sounds good, and don't say steak. You always want steak. I want something exotic," Shauny said and handed him his credit card back.

Abyle raised one dark brow. "Steaks are life, baby brat." He ruffled her hair.

They all agreed on a local mom and pop restaurant that catered to shifters, which also had a variety of meats. Atlas didn't care where they ate, if he got something in his empty belly sooner rather than later.

"We'll meet you both there after we drop off all this at the alpha house." Atika gestured toward his truck which was filled with packages.

After they'd agreed on the shopping trip, he and his twin had followed Atlas and Shauny into town. Their trucks both had lift kits that rivaled a monster truck. The bed of his was covered by a camper shell, making it perfect for concealing things. The matte black, custom Ford 350 Super-duty pickup had to cost over a hundred thousand dollars with all the custom parts. Abyle's grey pickup looked almost identical except for the main color and the lack of a camper shell. He wondered how his brothers had afforded such expensive vehicles, knowing their mother kept a tight hold of the family purse strings. He'd stayed away from home as much as possible since he'd turned eighteen, only stopping in for holidays. It had created a divide between Atlas and his siblings, but one that was necessary more so than a want.

When three sets of eyes seemed to bore into him, he pulled his focus back to the conversation. "Sounds solid. You need our help?" Fuck, for all he was aware, the alpha house needed to be cleaned out, possibly gutted. He scrubbed both hands down his face, feeling a days' worth of stubble. After his run through memory fucked-up-lane, they'd returned to the house he was supposed to call home. He'd crashed in the family room on one of the sofas, unwilling to sleep in the old alpha's bed.

"Nah, we got this. Get a table, and we'll meet you both there in less than a half hour. It'll probably take you that long to get seated," Abyle said.

He and Shauny handed the bags they held to his brothers, then they went to his SUV. "How're you really feeling today?" he asked holding the door open for her.

She took a deep breath but waited until he got behind the wheel to speak. "I'm still processing. I guess it hasn't really hit me yet. She wasn't in the house when it burned down last night. Like, why'd she burn her only home down and leave like that?"

Atlas tapped the wheel, thinking. "If she'd have stayed, she'd have been under my law. She knows I know what she did to me all those years ago. She watched me kill her husband and lover without trying to stop me. Not that she could've, but she was standing there watching him as he attempted to murder her son. Me,"—he pounded his fist on his chest—"It wasn't the first time she'd watched or participated when he punished me," he snarled. Old hate surfaced. How could parents have four children yet choose to hate just one? Not that he'd wish what he'd suffered on anyone else, but the crazy twisted mind of his parents freaked him out, making him question if those traits were passed on to him.

"There had been moments when I'd see the mother I always dreamed of. Mind you, they were few and far between, but when they appeared, they were awesome."

Shauny faced the passenger window, her pain twisting the image he could see in her reflection. "There was something wrong with her, not you or me, or any of us."

"You really believe that?" Her voice shook as she turned to face him.

Atlas nodded. For years he'd struggled with blaming himself. "Yeah, I really do. I was a seven year old cub, Shauny, what did I do to deserve the way they treated me? I mean, if I'd been the worst kid in the world, I still didn't deserve...that." His hand went to his chest and the non-existent scar.

His sister took a shuddering breath. "Goddess, you're right. Let's go get a table before two starving bears show up and demand answers," she said, trying for a lightness neither of them felt.

Before he put the vehicle in gear, he reached for her hand, the calluses on her palm speaking loudly of her hard work. "Things are going to be better for all of us." His words were a vow and a demand.

After a tense second, Shauny nodded, then he pulled his hand away, shifted into drive and headed toward the restaurant. Goddess, he prayed his promise could be upheld without too much bloodshed.

"Wow, this place is packed." Atlas sat back, staring at all the cars in the parking lot.

"It usually is since they cater to us shifters. They serve shifter pro-portion meals, meaning nobody leaves here hungry."

The times he'd come home, he hadn't stopped in town for much of anything, feeling accusing eyes on him not high on his list of things to do. "Time to face the firing squad," he quipped, hopping out quickly.

His feet were moving to the front of the SUV before he decided it was a bad idea, meeting Shauny who wore a bright grin.

"This is going to be fun, just wait and see." She grabbed his arm, dragging him toward the entrance.

"For such a sprite, you sure do have alarming strength," he grumbled.

The door opened as they stepped on the sidewalk, a well dressed male he recognized from the pack stood there along with a female, both wearing uniforms with the restaurant's name on a badge pinned to their chests. He stopped, forcing Shauny to jerk backward. "Afternoon," he rumbled, his bear pressing forward, always ready to protect.

"Good afternoon, Alpha. Are you here for dinner?"

Atlas thought that was a stupid question, since it was just past noon, and they were in the doorway to a restaurant but kept his expression neutral. "Yep. Got a table for four available?"

"The alpha table is always open, sir. Would you like to follow me? Um, you said for four?" The female asked, her green gaze looking behind him.

Shauny coughed, drawing the female's attention. "Our brothers will be joining us shortly."

"Oh, that's fine. Follow me, please." She ducked her head, not meeting Atlas's or Shauny's gazes.

The male gave a tip of his head, turning back to the podium, his hand picking up a pen and jotting down a note on the clipboard. Atlas didn't know about clan politics; had no clue the alpha had a standing reservation with a table always set aside for him. He waited for the young female to move away, after they were shown to their table, before asking Shauny if she'd known. "Has that always been the way of things, or was crazy Matty the one who demanded this?" He waved his hand to encompass the table they sat at.

"I don't know. It wasn't as if mother went to fancy restaurants after—well after she mated again. Especially since he wasn't named the alpha."

They both looked around the crowded restaurant, noticing everyone had turned to stare at them. Atlas and his bear wanted to roar at the lot of them. "Stay right here," he ordered Shauny, getting up before she could argue.

"Afternoon," he boomed. "Tomorrow night, I'd like to invite you all to the alpha house. Clearly, I'm new to the title, and as such, I'm going to be learning as I go, so I hope you all can bear with me. Pun intended." He grinned as many of the people in the room chuckled. "I only want to do what's best for the clan, but I also want to reassure you I'm just a man, who like all of you, will make mistakes. Now, if you have any questions, or issues, be sure and make an appointment through Shauny. She's going to act as my secretary for the time being. Alright, shows over, please enjoy your lunch." He smiled as the waitress hovered in the background, waiting to move forward.

He reached over the table, using two fingers to close Shauny's mouth. "You'll catch flies like that, sister dear."

"Are you two ready to order?"

"We're waiting on our brothers for the main course, but I'd like to get some appetizers and a beverage. How 'bout you?" He snapped his fingers, getting Shauny's attention.

"Did you just invite everyone to the house tomorrow and tell them all I was y...your secretary?" she sputtered.

Atlas flicked the napkin over his lap. "Yep."

Joni and Annie closed up the convenience store just as the final rays of the sun were setting. She couldn't remember the last time she actually felt like she'd accomplished something good.

"What's put that satisfied smile on your face?" Annie asked, walking next to her with her own satisfied grin for a whole other reason.

After Hollis had left, Joni couldn't help but know what they'd done for the forty-five minutes while the two had holed up in the office. Even if she'd not been a shifter, the look on Hollis's face when he'd walked out would've been a clear sign to any and all who'd seen him. His words of warning against talking to the creepy Mikey guy just before he'd left, weren't needed.

"I'll follow you home." Joni tossed her keys in the air, catching them easily.

Annie paused. "We should ride in together tomorrow. It seems silly for us to have two cars here and all." Her words were said gently, but they weren't exactly a suggestion.

Joni was used to dealing with alpha males, or rather steering clear of them. The alpha females she'd come in contact with had been her friends. Annie exhibited the same aura as Taryn and Sky, only on a different level. She wished she had a small bit of alpha bitch in herself, but then again, Keith would've beaten it right out of her long ago if she had, both mentally, psychologically, and probably physically as well. She shuddered; goosebumps rose all over her when a slight breeze blew past her. She swore she heard a man's voice whisper through the breeze, the sinister sound of his deep voice promising retribution.

"What's wrong?" Annie moved forward, facing Joni, her hands rubbed up and down Joni's arms while her head looked left and right.

At her touch, Joni jerked back, her fight or flight instincts kicked in. "Did you hear that?"

Annie looked around, her eyes widening while she inhaled deeply.

Goddess, she was losing her ever loving mind. Maybe she should've stayed in Mystic or entered one of the mentally insane facilities.

"I didn't hear anything, Vanessa. Are you okay? Did I work you too hard today?" Annie reached to touch Joni again, but then dropped her hands.

"No, I...I just thought. Never mind, it was probably just my imagination. Come on, I'll follow you home." Joni tried to sound convincing, tried to make her tone even and assured, but inside, her wolf didn't even rise. She wondered if she'd been in mortal danger if the stupid beast would come to her aid.

"You sure you're okay to drive?"

Joni nodded, not trusting her voice to be steady. Several beats passed before she spoke. "Yeah, I'm just a little tired. I think I'll skip dinner tonight and go to bed early if that's alright?"

Annie bit her lip but nodded. "I'm not your boss away from here," she assured her.

Following Annie's car gave her something to concentrate on, something other than herself and the strange voice whispering in the wind. Fog had creeped in, and with it a scary foreboding, if you believed in things that went bump in the night. Joni hadn't until she'd seen what Keith could become. Not many from their pack had truly seen the beast beneath the façade, but because she'd made a pact with the devil himself, she'd seen it. She shivered even though it was hot in Texas at night. She turned the heater on in the little beater car she'd bought, the warm air taking away some of the chill. "I'm so damn tired of being scared all the time."

The lights were all on at the big farmhouse, showing the silhouette of Hollis in the window, clearly waiting on his wife. Joni wished she'd had a mate, or even a man who loved her the way Annie and Hollis loved one another. Their love was a destiny that was sure to be denied to Joni forever. What she'd done, what she'd agreed to go through with Keith all in the name of friendship, had all but stolen her wolf. "I'd do it again a hundred times," she promised.

Instead of parking behind Annie, she maneuvered closer to the barn where they'd shown her to park, waving at Annie as she got out. "See you in the morning, Annie." Not waiting for a reply, she jogged up the stairway to the loft apartment, holding her breath the entire way in hopes the older couple didn't try to stop her. She just needed a night to regroup, a chance to take in all the changes to her life and even cry a little, silently of course.

Hollis stood by the entryway to the kitchen, waiting for his mate to come inside, the taillights of their guest's small vehicle headed toward the barn. "Where's Vanessa going?"

Annie placed her purse over the chair in the dining room as she walked in, her head turning toward the window. "Something spooked her tonight."

He straightened from the door. "Did you see or smell anything?"

His mate shook her head, then moved into his arms. "Someone hurt her, Hollis. I can feel it in here." She placed her small hand over her heart, looking up into his eyes like she thought he could fix it.

"I'm assigning one of the boys to watch over the shop for the next few days. Something doesn't feel right. I know she's a wolf, but she's suppressing her for a reason. Hell, if I wasn't an alpha, I don't think I'd have known what she was." He rubbed his hands up and down her back.

"Do you think she knows?" Annie asked, tilting her head back to look at him.

Everything stilled in him. "Shit, I didn't think of that. She runs like a gazelle, walks with the agility of a predator, and even tracks people with her eyes like one of us. Maybe that's natural, but you could be onto something. I'll introduce her to Thadd tomorrow, he's our best when it comes to things like this."

Annie pushed away. "I don't think so. Thadd is not going to interrogate that little girl." She stomped into the kitchen, the sound of pots and pans banging on the stove louder than usual.

Hollis sighed loudly before following. "I won't let Thadd interrogate her, just meet and talk as if he was stopping by for a quick chit chat. Believe me, I wouldn't hurt a little bit like her." He didn't mention unless she was a danger to his crew. He and Annie had been together for a very long time, taking in who others deemed lost or lost causes, but they were not too far gone that Hollis and his mate couldn't save them, couldn't salvage the humanity that was still within their beasts no matter what animal they were.

"I will be here when he stops for his chit chat, Hollis," she said, pointing a spoon dripping with spaghetti sauce at him.

He eliminated the space between them, covering her hand with his own while he dipped his head to taste the heavenly flavor of tomatoes and seasoning his mate had in the slow cooker all day. "Damn, Annie, you sure do know how to win a man through his stomach," he teased, licking his lips.

Annie raised a brow. "Well, you mess with that little girl out there, and that's the only thing you'll be eating for a long while, mister." She poked him in the chest with one finger.

"You know I'd only do what was best for you and our crew, darling," he whispered close to her ear.

"I know," she agreed. "There's just something broken about her." She sniffed as she turned back to the pot, putting pasta into the boiling water.

Hollis rested his head on top of hers. "There's always something a little broken in all our people. That's what makes them ours. We can only offer them a safe place to rest, help them heal, or let them realize their broken pieces aren't so bad. Being broken is part of life. You get back up and realize those pieces are now stronger, and sometimes even better, prettier than the smooth surfaces because they've got character, grit. There are way too many pretty people out there in the world. We need more folks like us with scars and cracks that've healed up. One day, she'll realize grit will get you a lot farther than pretty. Now, I ain't saying you're not gorgeous, 'cause I'd be damned if my dick doesn't still get hard at the sight of you, the smell of you 'cause, darling, I've never seen and never will see a woman more gorgeous than you. I've seen you, I know every inch of your body, and could tell you where you got that scar on the inside of your left thigh, but then, we'd have to put dinner off," he growled.

Annie shivered against him, her ass rubbing on his already extremely hard dick. Hell, he'd come running to the shop earlier, uncaring if Vanessa would be alerted, when she'd called out to him through their link as fast as he could, her fear at seeing Mikey the prick had his coyote seeing red. Now, his dick was up and ready to go like he'd not just been inside her hours ago.

"Are you hungry?" she asked.

Hollis turned her in his arms. "How long before the pasta is done?"

Annie looked at the boiling water. "It's done now."

He nodded, helped her drain the water, then maneuvered them both to the kitchen counter, smothering her giggle with his lips. "I'll teach you to tempt me, woman."

His mate raked her hands down his chest, ripping open the buttons on his flannel, the soft ping of the buttons flying across the room made him chuckle. "My mama always told me kitties were wild," he teased.

Annie purred, a sound he'd always love for the rest of their lives, then neither said anything for a long time while he made love to his mate, dinner forgotten as he claimed his wild cat.

Chapter Six

Joni couldn't sleep. A glance at the clock showed she'd gotten a total of four and a half hours sleep, and she was wired still. "At least I didn't have any bad dreams tonight," she muttered. She shoved the blanket back and walked to the huge window overlooking a cornfield. Never in her imagination did she think she'd live over a big red barn with a cornfield for a backyard, but there you go, life hands you lemons, you make a freaking lemonade or some shitting ass analogy.

She stretched her arms above her head, wincing at the pull of muscles. It had been almost two years since...well, since her last torture session with the evil bastard. At one time, she'd thought her parents were clueless to what had been going on. She'd tried so hard to hide her pain from them, going so far as to buy over the counter painkillers. Not that they did much, but when taken in the dosage she'd taken, they'd helped. Unlike her friend, she wasn't allowed to shift to heal. One of Keith's deals. However, he'd never said she couldn't take human medicine.

One day, after a particularly vicious beating Taryn had suffered, and in turn she'd had to suffer, Joni nearly wrecked her mother's car, driving into town for more meds. Goddess, the anger both her parents rained down on her could've been heard two counties over. She cringed thinking of the words that had come from her mother as her father sat in his favorite leather reading chair.

"Joni, what were you thinking, stupid girl. If you need pharmaceuticals that badly, you can ask me or your father, or just order them online. As much as that friend of yours gets her penance, I'd think you'd have a standing order," her mother said evenly.

"You...you know what he does to me, to T?"

Her father waved his hand, the sound of his paper rattled. *"It is none of our business. You made your bargain. You're lucky we don't tell him what you're doing."*

Joni met his cold brown eyes, seeing the truth of his statement in them. It would be nothing for them to tell Keith, their alpha, the daughter they were supposed to love was...taking painkillers after he tortures her. Goddess, she hated him and her mother. *"Ah, but if you do, I won't be able to do the job the two of you pretend you do, now will I. I mean, if I'm too hurt to get the fuck out of bed and all."* She turned at her mother's gasp, ignoring them both as she limped to her small bedroom at the back of the house. She didn't slam the door when she entered. She'd learned early on that would do nothing but create more hostility.

Her hand shook as she uncapped the ibuprophen bottle, taking six gel caps out even though that was probably too much for someone of her size. What doesn't kill you makes you stronger, she sang in her head, swallowing the green pills without any liquid. Her throat burned as they got stuck in her dry throat. She looked around the small space, finding a half empty bottle of Gatorade. *"No, the bottle is half full."* She chugged the contents, then went to lay down, hoping the little pills would dull the pain. Jeez, what the hell had Taryn gone through this time, she wondered. Her insides felt on fire, every single rib felt as if they'd been broken, and Joni was sure one of her lungs had been punctured, but thanks to her shifter ability, it had already begun healing by the time she'd gotten home. Fucking Keith was such a sadistic prick. He didn't even have to be in the same room as her to inflict the pain and injuries anymore. Now, all he had to do was connect through their 'private link' and bam, she was writhing on the floor, wishing for death.

A howl brought her back to the present, shaking her out of the painful past and things she couldn't change. "I can't change the past, and I can't seem to change into my wolf. I'm such a fucked up little whiner. No wonder Atlas left me." She wiped a tear from beneath her right eye.

Deciding she wasn't going to get anymore sleep, she headed toward the shower, stopping in the middle of the room. "Why shower if I'm going to go for a run? Oh, my gawd, I'm becoming one of those people.

I need to get a cat. Surely, I can get one of those since I'm not really a wolf." She slapped a hand over her mouth, trying to stifle her giggle without any luck. Finally, she gave up and amid laughter, she dressed in a pair of leggings and a T-shirt, putting on her running shoes that had seen lots of ground in both Mystic and Sturgis. After she made sure she had her phone and earbuds with music ready to play, she headed out, going the opposite way from before, not wanting to run into Oaklyn again. This time, she headed toward the road, feeling it was the safest area to travel on. The gravel was damp, which kept the dirt from flying up. She paced herself, watching for markers so she didn't get lost. At the end of the blacktop, she turned left, following the cornfield, assuming is was a mile marker.

Just as the sun was coming up, the yellow corn stocks to the right of her seemed to be swaying as if something big was moving through it since there wasn't a breeze. Joni was sure she heard a deep growl, but with her earbuds in, she couldn't be for sure. With one hand, she took the earbud closest to the moving stocks out, but kept running, her body poised to dart into the other field. Fucking fight or flight mode was her bestie for the restie.

Silence descended around her, even the air seemed to still. She knew all too well what that meant. A predator was in her vicinity, and she was most definitely the prey. Instead of stopping or yelling like a stupid scream queen in a movie, Joni picked up her speed and dodged into the field she was sure was owned by Hollis. Her finger was on the phone, dialing Annie before she'd realized what she was doing.

"Joni, you ready for breakfast?" Annie asked.

A growl rent the air.

"Annie, I need help," she screamed.

She could hear Annie hollering for Hollis but didn't think the other woman, or her husband were going to be able to help her, before whatever huge beast that was barreling toward her, got to her first. Still, she pumped her arms and legs, swatted at the dry leaves that smacked her in the face and arms, and ran for her life. "I didn't survive the fucking sadistic Keith to die in Wolfs Run, Texas by a...whatever is chasing me, dammit," she screamed, tripping over a root in the ground.

Before she could get up, warm breath fanned over her back as whatever had been chasing her landed with a thud on the other side, facing her with a loud snarl.

"If I click my heels three times, will it take me home?" Joni muttered not wanting to look up and see what it was that was going to eat her.

A huge paw landing an inch from her face, making Joni flinch. She peeked one eye open, finding a huge black and tan lion staring down at her. The big thing sat back, lifted his paw, then began to...oh good lord, was he? "Are you grooming yourself?"

The lion stood up and shook his huge mane, then sat back down like that made it better. "Are you someones pet?" Shit, now she was talking to lions in fields. "Am I already in the looney bin?" Hadn't she just said she could become a crazy cat lady earlier? Did owning a lion make her one?

The sound of feet, or paws, several if she wasn't mistaken, could be heard.

The lion tilted his head but didn't move. The corn stocks swayed, and then she was surrounded by—her mind couldn't quite process what she was seeing. She blinked several times, then opened her mouth. "Is this some kind of animal rescue?"

The air shimmered, and where once stood a coyote the size of a small grizzly bear, now stood Hollis with his arms crossed. "Thadd, I told you to come to the house for breakfast. What're you doing out here, scaring my guest?"

Joni looked at the lion, then at Hollis, then at the menagerie of animals. "I think I'm going to faint."

The lion shifted into one of the most gorgeous men she'd ever seen in her life, besides Atlas of course. He squatted down, his dick...right in her face. "Dude, dick in face is so not cool."

"Well, if you were going to pass out, you'd be fine, since you're already on the ground, and hey, if the last thing you saw was my cock, that's a bonus." He winked before he was shoved aside by Hollis, who was now wearing jeans.

"Here, let me help you up. I'm sure this is a lot to take in, and this was not how I wanted to do it," Hollis growled.

Thadd shrugged. "I was out for a run when she ran by. It's not my fault my cat wanted to play chase the mouse."

"Thaddaeus, come here." Annie wiggled her finger toward herself.

The big man, or rather lion groaned, but went over to Annie. She grabbed him by the ear as he got closer. "Don't you ever do that again, young man."

"Yes, ma'am. Do you know what she is though?"

All eyes turned to Joni, who stood there with wide eyes.

She bit her lip, waiting for them to ask.

Hollis crossed his arms.

"I can't shift. I mean, I used to be able to, but I can't anymore," she stammered, looking away so she didn't see the pity in their eyes.

"Well, I guess you need to get some training in then, don't cha?" Annie had released Thadd and come to her side. "You see, here in Wolfs Run, we are a crew. The Wilde Crew to be exact. We've got a little bit of everything. So, you're a wolf who can't shift...for the time being, maybe forever. Well then, you'll come to the gym after work and you'll learn how to defend yourself just like the cubs, kits, and other young. That's what being part of our crew means. We're family, and we protect our own, Vanessa." Annie clapped her hands together.

Joni looked around the gathering of people, no shifters, and realized these people were ready to accept her, a liar who couldn't shift. "My name is Joni," she whispered.

"Are there people who're gonna come looking for you that's gonna bring trouble here?" Hollis asked, his alpha aura flared.

Joni shook her head. "No. Nobody will miss me." The truth of her words made her chest ache, but she knew the other shifters around her could smell the honesty ringing in every word she said.

Thadd put his arm around her shoulders. "Well, you've now found several of us who would care. Of course, now that you're not gonna pass out...care to talk about my cock?"

"Thaddeus," Annie warned.

The lion laughed and jumped away as Annie snarled. "But, mama, I just wanna play," he whined.

"You keep your privates away from my girl, or I'll go online and buy one of those things that make it impossible for you to get an...erection." Annie shook her finger at him.

Several others had gathered by the barn, Joni noticed as they exited the field, and with their reactions, had to have overheard Annie's last words.

"Holy shit, did Annie just threaten Thadd?"

"Did Annie just say erection?"

"Somebody, get the smelling salts, Annie has said erection."

"That's enough. If I hear one more of you fools talk about my mate, and the word or anything to do with dick, cock, erection, or the likes, I'll personally cock block all your asses," Hollis growled.

Joni laughed as the huge men all put their hands over their dicks and walked away, backward.

"He wouldn't really, but isn't he sexy when he gets all alphalike?" Annie whispered.

Hollis bent to Annie's ear. "I'll show you just how alphalike I can be, tonight."

Joni laughed at the blush that covered Annie's cheeks, wishing she had a love like theirs.

"It'll have to be after I take Joni to the gym. I'll be all hot and sweaty, too." Annie batted her lashes, making Hollis groan.

"Woman, get your fine ass in the house before I..." Hollis cut off as Annie pulled Joni into the back door.

"That was so fun," Annie giggled.

"Um, he won't hurt you will he?" Joni looked out the window, watching Hollis speak with several men. Goodness, she went and landed herself not only amongst a group of shifters, but a group of mixed shifters. Maybe this was just where she needed to be. A misfit amongst misfits.

He was ready to rip every single clan members' head off with his bare hands. Shit, were they all a bunch of goddamn idiots? "No, you don't need to ask me for every little fucking thing," he swore, looking across the massive desk at his sister. A tick began to form behind his right eye. Hell, at this rate, he was sure he was going to be the first white bear to get a damn migraine.

"But, Alpha, the old...alpha's mate insisted we not make any purchases without her consent. Our money was clan money. If we needed anything, we were to ask her, and she—well, she had to release our funds. None of us have our own accounts." The young clan member on the other end stopped speaking.

Atlas put his head in his hands, staring down at the immaculate desk in front of him, wanting to destroy every inch of the room with his bare hands. "I'll be looking into returning everyone's money into their accounts. It never should've been put into one in the first place," he growled. Before he could say anything else that would taint Matilda's legacy further, not that the bitch deserved any loyalty, he hung up.

"Why the fuck was I not told this happened?" he asked Shauny.

His sister looked at him across the wood surface, her face shocked. "I had no clue. Mother never spoke of clan politics. I don't know if Atika or Abyle are aware either. They have their own money. I don't think they'd give it to the clan or were made to."

Atlas grabbed his cellphone, not trusting the landline in the office, then thought about bugs and who could be listening in on their conversation. Placing his finger to his lips, he opened his mind. *"What are the chances this place has cameras or listening devices?"*

"Matilda didn't know you'd be making her leave the way you did. I don't think she'd want any evidence of what she did in case someone did take over. Besides, if she had a camera or someway to listen in, she'd have to be close, right?" Shauny pretended to look over a book in front of her.

He thought about what she said, but still wasn't going to take any chances. With his senses open, the magic the Goddess had given him, he was attuned to electrical currents. If Matilda was relying on equipment, his bear would know. He stood, pretending to be deep in thought. "I don't know what to do, Shauny. How do we go about getting everyone the money they are due back to them?" He made a slow trek around his desk, then walked around the room, looking at the pictures, picking up different figurines and other things he was sure the old alpha hadn't put there. Once he was sure there wasn't anything that was recording them, he sat back with a sigh. "Okay, nothing I can detect. Now, I'm going to have to hire someone to go through the accounts and reverse every motherfucking penny to all the clansmen and women. This is going to take a long damn time." Shit, he didn't want to waste a minute on anything except going back to Mystic and claiming Joni.

"We've got trained clans' people who can do that. I can oversee them," Shauny offered.

At her offer, he raised a brow. "Explain?"

A blush stole up his baby sister's face. "Mother made sure I had schooling for things that she considered female's work. Accounting and

housework? I'm very well versed, but I would definitely need help doing what you need."

For the first time in twenty-four hours, he felt a tiny bit of relief.
"Get me the names of who you think would be the most helpful, and
I'll do a background check. How many do you need? They, of course,
will be paid," he growled. Nobody was going to be doing work for the
clan for free on his watch.

Shauny got up from her chair, walked around to his side of the desk
and wrapped her arms around his shoulders. "You're going to make a
great alpha."

Atlas felt her love and acceptance but wasn't sure she was right. A
part of him was missing, and that part was his mate, his forbidden wolf.
Even though he was alpha, he didn't think his clan would accept his
truemate was a wolf.

*****

Two Weeks Later...

"So, every clan member has their own account and what could be
returned to them has been, but that leaves the alpha account with very
little money." Shauny said as she entered his office.

Atlas sat behind the big desk, no longer quite so neat and pristine,
but it was now his. "Good," he said with satisfaction. He had his own
account with more than enough money.

Shauny plopped down in the chair across from him. "You realize
most alphas wouldn't have done what you did?" she asked.

He raised one brow. "Most alphas never would've done what had
been done here in the first place." He held up his hand when she went
to speak. "Well, any alpha worthy of the title. Now, tell me what's going
on in the clan." He'd been too busy untangling messes fucking Matilda had put them in with other clans to truly get into the politics of his
own clan.

"They all think you're a rockstar of alphas and can't wait for the party this evening, which is why I'm here. Why aren't you getting ready?" She tapped his desk.

He tugged at his beard, the one that had grown long enough for him to actually tug. "When did we plan a party?"

His sister grinned. "Well, you see, I figured since you've been such a good alpha, you needed to meet with the clan who loves you soo hard right now. Now, get your big bear ass up and go get clean and ready. While you're at it, shave that shit off your face and put on the new clothes that are laid out on your bed. Ps. I moved your stuff into the alpha suite." She raised her right hand as she stood. "I had it redone so there's no stink of crazy Matty to deal with. You're welcome." She laughed, turning on her tennis shoes and ran for the door.

Atlas shook his head at her antics. "One day, you're gonna find a mate who will put you over his knee and give you a good spanking, sister dear."

Shauny stopped with one hand on the door jam. "Pfft, there's not a bear in this clan who can handle this." She waved her hand up and down her frame.

He took in her appearance, shaking his head at what she wore. Only his sister could make a pair of black leggings with words written on them along with a white racerback tank, topped with a black cardigan, look expensive, but what he really wanted to laugh at was the tennis shoes that lit up as she walked. "Where the hell did you get those?" He nodded toward her.

She lifted her leg so that it was bent backward, her foot coming up to the side, almost touching her hip from behind. Damn female was flexible. "They're custom-made and spendy, brother. Thank you by the way," she teased.

"I'm assuming you expensed them?"

"Hey, I run here, there, and everywhere for you. I needed a good pair of tennis shoes. Gotta go get ready, and so do you." She pointed at him before letting her foot drop, the colors on the bottom shifting again.

"I'll be there. What time again?" he asked, shuffling papers around in front of him. He actually felt like he'd accomplished a lot in the two weeks he'd been there. When Shauny gave him the time, he nodded, made a note on one of the papers, then looked up when he felt her still staring at him. "What?"

"When you going to go get your mate?"

Stunned, he sat back, unable to believe she knew. "You better get going," he growled.

Unfazed by his tone, she crossed her arms and stared back at him. "You've got everything running like a pretty well oiled ship here. Atika and Abyle can keep things rocking while you do what your bear needs. After tonight, go do what you both need doing, or things will turn to shit for you."

She didn't wait for him to respond, just turned on her flashing shoes and left, closing his door on a quiet snick. Fuck, how the hell did she know? "Son-of-a-bitch," he swore.

Chapter Seven

Atlas looked around the large room, noticing the difference in the gathering from the last time they'd been here. Smiling faces greeted him. He raised the cut crystal glass to his lips, sipping at the bourbon, enjoying the slight burn. He didn't drink often and wouldn't drink much tonight. Even though as a shifter he wouldn't feel the affects much, he didn't like to have his mind fuzzy at all.

"How's it going, bro?" Atika asked, holding a bottle of beer in his hand.

"Good. How're you doing?" Atlas looked around the room, wondering where Abyle was. Usually where one twin was, the other was close.

"Abyle will be here shortly. We had some things to take care of before we moved in here for a short time. So, you ready for your road trip or what?" he asked, taking a sip of his beer.

Atlas growled. "How the hell you know I'm taking a trip?"

Atika placed a big palm on his shoulder. "Easy, Alpha, we're here if you do, and if you don't, we'll be here to have your back either way."

His brother's use of his title settled his bear, which pissed Atlas off at himself. He wasn't like his father, ready to tear the head off of anyone who stepped out of line. "Shit, I'm sorry, Atika."

Atika tipped his head back, swallowing the last of his drink. "You've got a lot on your plate."

"That gives me no right to snap at you. When the party's over, I need to talk to all of you before I decide to go after...before I leave." Whether he returned would be determined on how his siblings reacted to what his mate was. Atlas had already decided while he was getting ready, that Joni was his. He was going after her, and he would be claiming her. Coming back to the White Bear Clan as the alpha wasn't a set plan. He'd fixed the wrongs the old alpha's mate had done. In the hours after Shauny had left, he'd made a few choices of who'd take his place if the clan wasn't willing to accept Joni. In his mind, there was only one choice, or rather two. Atika and Abyle were more than enough bear to lead them. Hell, he knew for a fact they were as good if not better men, bears, than him.

"That sounds ominous, Atlas." Atika waived a waiter down, who was quick to come over, taking the empty bottle from him, promising to return with another.

"Not ominous, just some real talk that should've been done weeks ago," Atlas said. He searched the crowd for Shauny and Abyle, relaxing when he spotted both of them chatting with groups of members he recognized.

Throughout the night, he accepted more thanks and back slaps than he could count. Hell, he wasn't sure how many cubs he kissed. At one point, he almost had a cub throw up on him and even had one female ask him if she could name her unborn after him. "Ah, I think you should name him after someone who is part of your family," he suggested.

"You are part of our family, Alpha." She teared up. "You...you don't know how much it means to my family what you've done. Words can't express our gratitude," she gushed.

Atlas didn't know what to say, luckily Shauny had overheard and saved him. As the last guest left, he felt...drained. He hadn't done anything a good alpha wouldn't have done. "Thank fuck that's over." He walked into his office, or rather the alpha office. It was possible that after he told the others what his plans were they'd all agree he wasn't good enough for the position, or that they wouldn't accept Joni.

"Have a seat," he suggested, waving his hand toward the sofa and chairs situated off to the side of the room. He grabbed the bottle of bourbon he preferred and four glasses. "I think we'll all need a drink, and Shauny, you'll have one, too."

"Well, if I grow hair on my chest, it'll be your fault I don't find a mate," she teased, taking the glass he offered.

"Give her a double," Abyle said, accepting his own glass and passing Atika one.

Atlas poured them each a hefty serving, then poured one for himself before taking a seat in the last chair. He looked at his twin brothers who sat side-by-side on the leather sofa, then glanced at Shauny in one of the leather chairs. "I'm not sure how much you know about my search for my truemate, but I found her in Mystic, South Dakota." He swallowed before continuing. "Her name is Joni, and she's a wolf."

Silence greeted his statement.

"I like her name," Shauny finally said.

Abyle raised his hand. "Why didn't you claim her and bring her back here with you?"

He shook his head. "What the fuck?"

"If she's your truemate, why didn't you bring her back here and tell Matilda to shove her shit up her ass?" Atika asked.

A snort escaped Abyle, which made Atika laugh. "Alright, I guess shoving shit up Matilda's ass would be hard, but you get my meaning," Atika corrected.

"Matilda is a fucked up bitch. She'd have found some law or rule before I took the alpha title, and either killed Joni outright, or made it to where I wasn't alpha. I had to play by her rules first," he argued.

Shauny nodded. "I agree. However, I didn't know she was bringing the girl here first. That was a shocker for me. I'd been keeping tabs on the alpha house, but yeah, that was a twist I hadn't seen. So, now what?"

His mind reeled at their words. "You're all okay with the fact my truemate is a wolf?"

Abyle downed his drink, placing it on the end table next to him. "The Goddess has blessed you with a truemate. You have any clue how lucky you are? Any of the fuckers in the clan has a problem with that, then they'll face us. If they want you out of the clan, then we're all out. Let them find a new alpha who can do what you've done in two fucking weeks. The old alpha, hell, just about any other alpha, would've stepped in, would've seen the amount of money and power they had at their fingertips, and would've kept it for themselves."

Atlas squinted at his older brother. "Not you or Atika. You both would've done the same as I did," he argued.

Abyle and Atika nodded, but it was Abyle who spoke up. "We would've tried, but they wouldn't have followed us. We're not the white bear that was prophesized. We don't blame you for your heritage. Hell, I always felt a little sorry for you. If I'd have known what you'd gone through," he choked back an angry growl. "If we'd known what they'd done to you...I wish I could've been a better protector to you when you were a cub. I vow to be better from now 'til the end of time." He pounded his fist on his chest.

Atika repeated the words, letting him know that no matter what the clan said they'd go where he led.

"I'm with you three, and after you claim Joni, she'll be my sister as well. We'll make our own clan if we have to." A smile lit up her face. "I have a feeling that won't happen, though. This clan, our clan, loves you and what you did for them when you didn't have to."

He wasn't so sure, but whatever the future held, he was claiming Joni. Forbidden or not, she was his. Now he just needed to beg her forgiveness and pray she agreed.

"Well, I guess I'm going to need to go woo one reluctant wolf and hope like hell she doesn't rip my head off for leaving her."

"You're too tall for her to rip your head off," Atika said with a laugh.

Atlas wasn't too sure if that was true, his mate was a resourceful female. He didn't realize just how true his last thought was until the next day when he rolled into Mystic South Dakota, only to find she'd left without a trace.

****

"What the hell do you mean you have no fucking clue where one of your pack members went? Don't you have a link with them?" he roared in Niall's face. The alpha of the Mystic Wolves didn't flinch at his show of dominance.

"Bear, I suggest you slow your roll before you and I get into a tumble neither of us want." Niall's wolf pushed at Atlas.

In a fight, Atlas knew he was the bigger, badder, Apex predator, both in size and dominance. He was not only a bear, but a white bear that was three times the size of a normal grizzly, but he was on wolf territory alone. Wolves fought in a pack, and this wolf in front of him was the alpha. If he fucked with him, he'd be taking on the entire Mystic Pack. With effort, he reigned in his temper. "I apologize for my outburst, but you must understand she's mine," he gritted out between his teeth.

Niall raised his brows. "Really? I don't smell a mating on you, nor did she come to me with a request. As a matter of fact, I don't remember getting a request for you to come onto my pack lands at all."

Atlas was an alpha like Niall and knew the other man had a point. However, he'd not come onto pack lands for that reason. He'd been searching for his truemate, knowing as the white bear he'd be taking on the title of alpha. Intuition had drawn him to the small town of Sturgis, where he'd seen the gorgeous female Joni. She'd told him about her pack, but he'd never gone up to Mystic lands, until today, which he told Niall.

"So, you're telling me in all the time you'd spent with one of my pack, you and she never came on our lands?" Niall poked a finger toward Atlas.

He stood to his full height, towering over the alpha wolf. "I may be many things, including a dumbass for not claiming her when I was here, but a liar I am not," he growled.

A small grin split Niall's lip. "I think you and I will get along just fine. Come on, let's grab a beer inside, my mate is yelling at me for being a dumbass."

Inside Niall's house, Atlas couldn't help but notice the difference between it and the one back at White Bear Clan. Here, the house was a home, instead of a show place. A young boy came running around the corner, his eyes widening when he saw Atlas.

"Yikes, you're huge. What are you?"

Atlas squatted down. "I'm a bear," he said, holding out his hand.

"I'm Nolan, and I'm a wolf. Nice to meet you, Mr. Bear."

He shook the boy's hand. "Whatcha got there?"

The kid held up the electronic device. "It's my video game. I get to play with people all over the world, but there's this one player who I think is a girl. She totally kicks everyone's butt, but I think she's from America. Her name is Pleione, which is an odd name, but whatever, she totally kicks—butt," he paused, looking at Niall before continuing. "Dad, can I go to grandpa and grandma's tonight?"

Atlas froze at the name of the female character's name. In ancient history, Pleione was the name of Atlas's wife. "Niall, did Joni play video games?" he asked the alpha.

Niall paused at answering his son. "I don't really know, man. Her history is kind of messed up. I'd have to ask Taryn or Sky. Why do you ask?"

He shook his head, looking at Nolan then at Niall. "What's the name of the game you're playing?" he asked Nolan instead of answering Niall.

Nolan named a popular game, one that even he, who didn't play himself, had heard of. Atlas nodded, tried for a smile. "Very cool."

"Go ask Alaina if it's okay for you to go?" Niall ruffled his son's hair.

Atlas waited for the kid to run out of the room, his joyous woop floated back to them, then he reappeared. "Mom said I could go as long as my room is clean."

"Well, is it?" Niall asked.

"Duh," Nolan quipped, before jumping into his dad's arms. "Love you."

The genuine warmth of the home made Atlas long for the same thing. Once the cub had gone, he and Niall settled down in the comfy living room, the alpha's mate having waddled in with tears in her eyes. "He called me mom."

Clearly, the cub hadn't done that before. Niall had taken a few minutes with his mate while Atlas let his bear closer to the surface. Not that he planned to shift, but his animal could detect things that he as a man couldn't. Joni hadn't been to the alpha's home, or if she had it hadn't been recently. Not a single trace of her could he detect.

"Sorry about that," Niall said with a happy sigh. "My son loves Alaina, but he's never called her mom before now. She's pregnant, which obviously makes her even more emotional." He sat back with a grin.

"I'll show you emotional," Alaina hollered from the other room.

"And obviously has no issues with her hearing. Love you, mate." Niall shifted, placing one foot on top of his other knee, a casual pose. "I can feel your bear. Now, tell me what you know about my pack member, Joni." The order was made casually.

Atlas narrowed his eyes, sitting forward. "Where is she?"

Niall placed both feet on the floor, all sense of ease gone. "A few weeks ago, she up and left without a goodbye to anyone and nobody has seen her since. A week ago, she contacted Sky and Taryn, her two best friends, and let them know she was safe and from what they said, happy. Now, what the fuck did you do that made her run?"

His bear bristled at the accusation, but then he sat back, stunned. He'd left, that's what he'd done. Had his leaving been the reason she had run as well? "I need to talk to her friends. Maybe she gave them a clue or told them where she was." Desperation laced his tone but he didn't care. He'd get on his knees and beg if he had to.

"I'll need to ask their mates first." Niall let out a weary sigh. "I'm afraid that's going to be easier said than done. While Taryn might have a more amiable mate, Sky on the other hand...you might have an easier chance asking the sun not to rise in the morning," he warned.

Atlas tilted his head to the side. "Why is that?"

"Well, it might just be easier to show, rather than tell. Come on, let's get to it then." Niall stood up. Alaina, I need to call a small pack meeting. You going to be okay for a few hours?"

Alaina came into the room, her hand on her distended stomach. "I think this one and I have an understanding. She's to stay put for another month, or she's grounded for the next twenty years."

Niall pulled his mate into his arms. "I'm pretty sure that's not how it works. In fact, if it did, Nolan would still be grounded."

Atlas turned away, giving them a little privacy. Alaina looked as though she was ready to give birth at any moment, the poor female. He wasn't sure how mother nature, or the Goddess, worked, but was happy as all get out males weren't the ones who had to carry the young. Not that he didn't think females weren't gorgeous while they were pregnant. In fact, he thought they were even more radiant, but if he was honest, he didn't think males could handle labor and delivery, let alone nine months of carrying another inside them.

"You ready? Jett said we could come on over to his and Taryn's place since his mate and Sky are together, and Sky's mates have agreed to meet us there." Niall waved toward Atlas's Escalade. "You want to drive or ride with me?"

Atlas paused. "Mates, as in plural?"

"You got a problem with that?" Niall asked with a growl.

"Not at all. If the Goddess has paired them, who am I to judge?"

Niall slapped him on the shoulder. "Good bear."

The other wolf's home was what he'd expected, but the wolves were a little standoffish, which he supposed shouldn't have surprised him.

"What do you want with our girl, Atlas?"

Atlas recognized the female as Sky. Joni had pointed her out when they'd been at the movies together. She'd been hurt when the other female hadn't spoken to her, but Atlas had been secretly glad to have had the alone time with Joni. The last thing he'd wanted to do was spend their time together chatting with others. When he felt the others staring at him, he quickly shook himself from the memory. "She's my mate," he stated.

"Then why the fuck did she run away without a word to any of us, and why did you not mate her while you were here before leaving for parts unknown?" Taryn growled.

As the two women got agitated, Atlas felt their mates' wolves pushing at them. His bear raked at him to show them just who was the dominate shifter in the room, but he pushed the beast back. "I come from a clan that isn't, or rather wasn't as open to mixed pairings as yours. I had to make some changes before I could...claim Joni. I didn't want to endanger her."

A deep, rumbling growl, much fiercer than any female bear, came from the tiny female named Sky. "Whoever thinks to harm Joni has to go through me and my beasts."

The two men standing next to her placed a hand on her shoulder, trying to calm whatever was inside her.

"Down, girl," Taryn said with a grin. "If your outdated clan think to harm one hair on our besties head, I promise you, they'll be sorry."

Atlas smiled. "Duly noted and appreciated. However, before I took over as alpha, I wasn't sure how the wind blew up there. Trust me when I say it was a shitshow. Now, all that is meaningless if we don't know where Joni is." Frustration ate at him.

Sky sighed. "I think that's partly our fault, too. We, all of us, kept secrets. Her parents are assholes of the tenth degree. When I finally pulled my head out of my ass, I'm ashamed to say she'd been gone for a couple days, at least. Her egg and sperm donors seemed just as oblivious as us that she'd flown the coop, or so they said. When I pressed them as to her whereabouts, they became frantic. Like, holy-fucking-shit where the hell did she go frantic, or holy-fucking-shit I need a really good story, or the dragonish girl is going to eat me." Sky sighed, then looked down at the floor before she continued in a subdued tone. "I think Joni kept secrets from all of us. I've looked for her, but she's kind of a tech genius, similar to her parents. That was why Keith kept them in the positions they had."

Atlas listened to Sky and Taryn outline what they knew of Joni and her family. Hearing how they were the web masters of the old pack gave him chills. His mate could've virtually and physically disappeared with a new identity, leaving him with no way to trace her. "Fuck me running," he muttered.

Sky gasped. "Um, I might have an idea, but I have to warn you, she's a wee bit strange."

"I'm willing to try anything," he reassured her.

Niall groaned. "Are we calling on Jenna or Lula?"

"Hey, you got a frog in your pocket, or am I doing the calling?" Sky grinned.

"Little girl, you're getting awfully big for your britches. I think your mates need to take you in hand." Niall growled, crossing his arms over his chest, his alpha powers flaring over the room, making Sky and the others fall to their knees.

"Damn, Niall," Raydon groaned, reaching for Sky.

"Sorry, Alpha." Sky raised her purple eyes to Niall, then tilted her head to the side in apology.

Niall must've pulled his powers back as all the wolves sighed. "I think Sky meant to say she was going to reach out to Lula since Jenna was handling some family business with her mates, right, hellmouth?"

Sky's eyes flashed a brighter purple, but she nodded. "Lula said she'd be here shortly."

A shift in the air had Atlas looking around the room, then he noticed a petite female with pink hair appearing out of thin air.

"Well, would you look at that," the female said, walking toward him. She sniffed the air. "Oh, he smells like alpha bear, looks like alpha bear, but he's more. Holy buckets batman, we gots a dire bear in the room." She paused a foot from him. "Niall, you're a brave alpha to allow one such as him so close to your pregnant mate."

Niall growled low and loud. "What the fuck do you mean a dire bear?"

The other wolves moved behind him, creating a wall of what, Atlas didn't know. Hell, he'd never heard of himself, or any other white bear being referred to as such a thing. "What the hell you talking about, female?"

Lula bristled. "I'm a dragon, dire bear, not just a female. You may be big and bad, but I can eat you for breakfast," she warned.

"Fuck me running," he swore.

"Nah, you're not my type, besides, who fucks and runs besides bunnies. They might, but I don't really know because well, they're bunnies, and I eat them, but only if I'm really hungry and...what? What did I say?" Lula turned to stare at the wolves.

"Lula, tell me you don't eat the Easter Bunny?"

"Stop it, everyone," Niall roared.

Chapter Eight

Joni fell back on the mat. "Okay, that's enough. Seriously, Annie, I can't hang," she panted. They'd been hitting what Hollis and Annie called the Gym for the past week, working with the shifters of the Wilde Crew in human form. Joni hadn't thought she'd like another pack as much as she'd liked the Mystic pack, but this Crew, was really close. They were a bunch of misfits, or lost ones, who came together as a family more so than anything else.

"So, why does your wolf hide?" Annie asked, taking a sip from the water bottle.

She stilled, fear skating over her. In the time she'd been with them, not once had they pushed her to talk about her past, other than to ask if she would be bringing trouble to their door. After she'd reassured them she wouldn't, they'd nodded and welcomed her like she was one of their own. A glance across the huge space showed nobody was paying any attention to her and Annie. Although she knew if she put one foot wrong, any one of the shifters would be there in an instant to protect Annie should the need arise. "My old alpha, not the one who...I just left. Shoot, that sounds weird. The alpha I grew up having to bow and scrape to was a sadistic asshole. No, he was worse than that. He was an evil bastard who took great pleasure in others' pain. I won't go into the details of his deeds, suffice to say, he...the things he did to another physically, I bargained with him, in order for me to be able to help her afterward. She was his daughter and one of my best friends. He tortured her, physically. I didn't realize he could do the same to me without actually laying a finger on me. So, after she healed, I would then suffer the same, only I couldn't let anyone know. Which was easy because nobody saw me most of the time. My family's job was to surf the internet, literally, and make the pack money by finding the right places to invest, then keeping the accounts for the pack. Keith fucked with black magic and that's all I'm going to say on that."

Her voice shook at the end, the memories of all the times she couldn't get out of bed. The broken bones, the ruptured organs, all the things poor Taryn had faced at the fist and feet of her father. Goddess, how awful it had been to witness her friend's suffering. Her saving grace was she'd been able to prepare, had been able to order supplies for herself, while Taryn had to limp back to her tiny room alone, save for Joni and Sky. That was the compromise she'd made with Keith. He had agreed to allow them to care for Taryn, in exchange for Joni taking the same punishments. Oh, he hadn't shown up and doled out the abuse in physical form. He'd been powerful enough he could do it through their private mental link. Her wolf had tried to stop him at first, but he'd beaten the poor beast into submission too many times, now she couldn't feel her, not even when she needed her, not even now that Keith was dead and gone.

"You see, I don't think my wolf is here anymore. When she needed me, I was too much of a coward to help her. I allowed him to hurt us, so she retreated," she whispered her deepest fear.

Annie wrapped her arms around her. "No, honey, you're not. You're the farthest thing from a coward I've ever known. You, you're a warrior and a protector. Even if your wolf never comes out again, you'll always be a warrior female. Now, come on. Let's head out, and we'll pick something up for dinner. I'm too tired to cook."

Joni let Annie help her stand, but her words helped her lift her shoulders a little higher. Learning to use the extra strength her shifter side gave her to fight also gave her a little hope she could protect herself if she needed. She didn't kid herself thinking she could win if she went up against another shifter, but at least she could put up a good fight.

"I don't give a fuck if she eats damn Bambi, if she can find Joni for me," Atlas growled.

Lula clapped her hands, then twisted her long pink hair into a bun, several bobby pins appearing in her mouth. When she was done, she smiled. "I knew I liked you. And just for the record, I don't eat Bambi. Baby deer have spots and they freak me out. Okie dokie, now give me a minute." She walked away, spinning on impossibly tall wedges, her tu-tu like skirt fluffing out, showing off boy shorts underneath. The female looked more like an anime character than a real life female, but he kept his thoughts to himself. She was almost too gorgeous for reality.

Lula turned, gave him a wink, then spun again, doing a walk around the room, her hand touching different things in the room. As she stopped behind Jett and Taryn, she paused. "You two are just sooo darn sweet. I see a great future ahead of you, but really, magic Jett, you need to stop with the worrying. There are no baby planks running around out there. This one will be your only baby mama drama you'll need worry about for the rest of your lives." She slapped his ass. "Now that doesn't mean the rest of the women shouldn't get to enjoy your dancing skills every now and then. Taryn, be a sweetie and let him be a good male dancer, like once a month, just so the other men can get laid as their women pretend its him they're doing, Mystic men aside." She winked.

"My mate doesn't need to see him bump and grind to get horny," Niall groused.

"Of course, she don't, duh." Lula rolled her eyes. "Now, you want to know where Jonessa is, yes?"

Atlas shook his head. "No, her name is Joni." He looked at the pink haired dragon female, worrying they might have called in a crazy one.

She wagged her finger at him. "Crazy is as crazy does, dire bear. Your female is a smart one. You see, she went clickity clack on her computer and zip zing zang, she has a new identity. Joni is now Vanessa, i.e. Jonessa." She waved her hand in the air and took a bow.

Niall pinched the bridge of his nose. "So, can you tell us where…she is?"

Lula lifted one shoulder. "I can."

They all stared at Lula, who stared back.

"Oh, you want me to tell you where she's at?"

This time Atlas couldn't keep his growl contained; his bear pushed closer, white fur rippled over his forearms. "Female, tell me where to find my mate. Please," he grated.

"Why is it that in all the stories they make you bears all soft and cuddly, but in reality, you're all big, bad, and snarly," she tsked. "Fine, I'll show you where she is." She waved him forward.

"Lula, be nice," Niall implored.

"Lula be nice," she mocked in a sing-song voice. "Lula, don't eat this, don't eat that. Lula, don't do this, don't do that. You all are the killers of fun. Pfft. I might as well have stayed in the Fey Realm and listened to my dragon mother, or better yet, stayed an egg," she complained.

Sky held her hand up. "Do dragons hatch from an egg, then?"

"I don't think we really want to know, hellmouth."

"River, I totally want to know. I have a bit of dragon in me. What if I have an egg?"

"You will not have an egg, dragon or no. You're pups will be all wolfies or maybe wolfagons, since a dragolf sounds weird." Lula looked at the trio, then at Atlas. "Now, come, I'll take you to Jonessa."

"Her name is Joni," he growled.

"Potaytoe, Poe tot toe," she said.

"I suggest you just go and not tug the tail of a dragon, Atlas." Niall shook his head.

"Why would you tug my tail? Does he not know a dragon's tail, while magnificent, is also very dangerous actually? Dire bear, it would be incredibly stupid of you to tug my tail, or any dragon's, tail," she warned, snapping her fingers. "Come, time is wasting, and danger is getting closer to the female."

Her words had him hurrying over to her. "What do you mean?"

"Bye, my furry friends, I will see you soon. Niall, your mate is in need of you. Your wolfie pup wasn't willing to wait the month she demanded, silly girl. Ps. Lula Junior is an awesome name, just saying." She grinned, then grabbed Atlas's arm. "Let's go, dire bear."

Atlas looked at the stricken face of the alpha, but before he could say his goodbyes, he and the crazy dragon were gone. "Motherfuck," he muttered.

Atlas fell on his ass in the middle of a cornfield, stocks falling beneath his weight. "What the hell, female?" he groaned, falling backward, staring up at the starry sky.

"Ah, doesn't it smell wonderful? Take a deep breath, dire bear. Tell me, what do you smell? And if you say something like shit, I will personally kick you in the nads." Lula sat beside him, or rather flounced down, her fluffy skirt of tulle covering half his face.

"How old are you, female?" He shoved the material off his face pushing to a sitting position, his arms hanging over his knees to look over at her.

"Ah, much older than you, dire bear," she assured him.

"My name is Atlas, female," he growled.

She got up, dusting off her skirt. "And my name is Lula, dire bear." He nodded. "Touché, Lula." He held out his hand. "Friends?"

"Frenemies," she agreed.

Atlas laughed. "Why are we enemies?"

"You're a dire bear, that comes with great responsibilities. Until you mate, you're a liability to all other shifters. My friends are shifters." She turned in a circle. "Your female is that way, but we have company coming in from that way." Lula held her fingers up, counting off. "Three, two, one."

A huge lion with a black mane leapt out, followed by a wolf and a grizzly bear. Lula clapped as if she was excited, but Atlas growled, shifting into his bear, roaring loudly. All the animals in front of him skidded to a stop, their paws digging into the ground, tearing down the cornfield around them when they tried to find purchase.

"Aw, come on, fight, fight, fight," Lula cheered.

Atlas swung his head toward her. In his bear form, he towered over them all, the top of Lula's head a good foot or so below his shoulder when he was on all fours. If he stood on his hind legs, his massive grizzly stood at close to twenty-two feet tall.

"What the hell are you?" A booming voice called from behind him.

Although he was irritated with the female dragon, his bear moved to protect her, placing his body between her and the newcomer. His bear growled.

"And just like that, we became friends instead of frenemies," Lula said, clapping. Her hand tugged on his fur. "Now, be nice to the alpha. He's kinda got an in with your female," she whispered loudly.

"Boys, shift back. I think it's pretty safe to say, if he wanted to eat us all, he could, and well, Pinky Tuscadaro over there would probably help, or cheer him on."

"Although it goes against my better judgement, I'm going to give them all clothes." Lula snapped her fingers. "How do you like that?" she asked.

Atlas in bear form turned to look over his shoulder, seeing the shifters turn into men, their bodies seamlessly shifting and being clothed in...*good goddess*, he definitely planned on staying on Lula's good side. The booty shorts she gave the men to wear with tassels dangling off the bottom could only be classified as stripper attire. Not that he had anything against strippers in general, but damn, he was sure the males standing with their hands over their dicks weren't at all happy with the spandex she'd given them.

"Can I keep these?" the man he had seen as the huge lion asked.

The one who'd ordered them to shift growled, but the lion shifter laughed. "Hey, my future mate would totally love these." He shook his hips back and forth, making the tassels move.

Lula raised her hand. "I agree."

Atlas shifted; energy swirled around him along with the knowledge on how to clothe himself after a shift. He made sure he wore what he would normally wear when facing an alpha and his future mate. His big hand came up and covered Lula's eyes. "You do not need to see that male doing that, Lula." He glared at the stupid lion. "Go home and put some clothes on, all of you." He pushed out his own alpha powers, not shocked when they all averted their gazes, turning to do as he said.

The alpha male grunted but didn't say anything when his people had turned tail. "Neat trick, son. Now, why don't you tell me why you and Pinky here decided to decimate a large swath of my crops?"

Lula raised her hand, but Atlas still held his hand over her eyes. "I apologize for the damage we did here. I assure you it wasn't our intent, and any money you might lose, I will repay plus interest."

"What's your name?"

"I'm Atlas. I'm looking for my mate Joni." He saw no reason to lie or beat around the bush.

"Well, if you think I'm just going to hand her off to just anyone, you better think again." He inhaled, staring into Atlas's eyes. "Come on, let's head back to my house. We'll see what the women think. If Joni or my mate take issue with either of you, huge ass bear and whatever Pinky here is not withstanding, you'll have to go through my crew first," he warned.

Lula clapped. "More frenemies."

Atlas sighed. "Come on, crazy." He tugged her along with him.

"Crazy is as crazy does," she repeated.

"Do you think they're okay?" Joni bit her lip, fear for Hollis had her looking out the window again. Annie and Hollis had each felt some sort of call, but since she wasn't an official member of their crew, she'd not heard or felt what it was. It didn't mean she wasn't worried for her friends.

"Hollis said all was fine and is on his way back. He said to warn you he's bringing someone from your past here." Annie's eyes held a bit of anger.

Joni turned from the window. "What?"

"You said nobody would come looking for you here. Did you bring trouble to our crew?" Annie crowded her against the counter.

"No. I promise. Nobody would care if I lived or died from my old pack." Keith was dead. Her parents were set up and didn't need her for the finances. Why would anyone be looking for her?

"You're telling the truth, or at least to your knowledge. I'm sorry, Joni. These are my people," Annie said.

The fact that she wasn't considered one of her people hit Joni, hard. "I'm aware, Annie. I've always been aware," she bit out.

"I didn't mean it like that." Annie reached out to her, but Joni flinched away.

The back door opened, saving Joni from hearing more platitudes. She was stupid thinking they'd accept her as one of theirs. She couldn't shift. She couldn't add to the crew, not like the others. Sure, she helped set their computers up, got the store computers working smoother so that Annie could find and order things easily, but anyone with half a brain could've done what she did.

Her breath stalled at a scent she thought she'd never smell again. Her eyes widened at the big man who followed Hollis inside, his gorgeous blue eyes met and held hers. Everything inside her stilled. Even the stupid wolf inside her seemed to wake up and hold her breath. "Atlas," she whispered.

"Jonessa," Lula cheered.

At the strange name, she jerked her eyes to the female dragon behind Atlas. "Um, Lula, what are you doing here?"

"Oh, ya know, being the fairy dragon to you and this dire bear. What are you doing here?" Lula asked, strolling into the kitchen, touching the different things Annie had on display. "Ah, you must be Annie, the lady of the house. I've smelled so much about you." Lula grabbed Annie's hand, pumping it up and down, up and down, several times before releasing her.

"Err, you mean, heard?" Annie asked.

Lula let go of Annie's hand, tapping her nose. "Nope, smelled. So, whatcha doin?" Lula asked, plopping down on a kitchen chair, crossing her legs, putting her arms over them as she stared around the space.

Joni looked between Lula and Annie, then to Atlas. "Um, what's going on?"

He shrugged. "I went to Mystic, had a chat with Niall, and then Lula agreed to help me find you."

Her friend Annie looked as if she'd swallowed saw dust and hadn't drank a lick of water in days. Joni took a closer look, her wolf seemed to surface a little more. "Annie, are you okay?"

"Yeah, I'm fine," Annie assured her after coughing a few times.

Even without her wolf, Joni could smell the lie. However, Hollis pulled Annie into his side. "Joni, you don't have to talk to him, or do anything you don't want to. I know you haven't formally joined my crew, but that doesn't mean I don't—we don't consider you one of ours."

Atlas growled; the sound had the hair on her arms standing up. "Thank you, Hollis. Um, can we have a few minutes to talk...in private?"

Lula sighed. "Isn't lost love a beautiful thing?" She leaned against the counter, snatching up an apple, tossing it in the air with one hand, catching it in the other. "Who wants to play a game of catch?"

"Lula, Niall said to tell you to play nice," Atlas warned.

The female dragon widened her purple eyes, looking way too innocent. "I always play nice. It's the idiots who are stupid that don't." She looked around the room. "Are there any idiots in residence here?"

"Female, you're in my home. I suggest you watch your tone," Hollis barked.

Lula stood straight. All act of joviality gone. "Joni, why don't you take Atlas up to the barn and have a little chit chat while I have one with Hollis and Annie here?"

"Um, why don't you come with us?" Joni suggested.

"Nah, you two need a little alone time to work some things out. We'll be fine. Won't we?" Lula looked at Hollis who still had his arm around his mate.

"I agree. My crew is close." Hollis's warning was clear to all. If Lula did anything that Hollis didn't like, the Wilde Crew would be there to protect them. What Joni wanted to tell them was that Lula cold decimate them all with only a blink and a breath of fire.

"Come on, Lula will be fine. She's given her word she'll be nice," Atlas promised.

Chapter Nine

Atlas wanted to sweep Joni up into his arms when he walked into the house. Common sense kept him in check, marginally. His bear snarled as they waited for her to agree to go with him. Although leaving Lula alone with the alpha and his mate might not be the smartest thing, he knew the dragon wouldn't kill them. He hoped. However, whatever she smelled coming from the female Annie would determine her fate once Lula finished interrogating her.

"Lead the way, Joni." He knew where she'd been staying. Her scent was everywhere, making his bear crazy. However, the strongest place was above the barn not too far from the main house. Luckily for all of them, there were no males, other than Hollis, who he could detect having come and gone from there recently.

Joni jerked her eyes up to his, her green eyes weary. "Why are you really here?"

Her question startled him. "What do you mean? I came as soon as I settled things at home. I'd have come sooner if things weren't such a shitshow, and I'd have known it was safe to claim you sooner."

"Bullshit. You could've claimed me before you left. You knew I wanted you," she gasped, covering her mouth with her hand. "Forget I said that." Joni hurried up the stairs.

He wouldn't allow her to run from him, not again, not ever. With speed, he swept her off her feet and into his arms, taking the stairs two and three at a time. "Put me down, you big oaf." She beat at his shoulder ineffectually.

"Sweetheart, you can hit me, bite me, hell, even claw me if you'd like, but I won't be putting you down until we get a few things settled." He shifted her so that one hand was free, and he could open the door without breaking it down.

"Does this whole barbarian thing work with the ladies?" she asked, her green eyes shooting sparks up at him.

Atlas tugged her the scant inches closer so that their noses were almost touching, her breath fanning his face. "I wouldn't know. You're
the first female I've ever almost had to kidnap," he teased.

Her intoxicating scent flared, sweet orange and roses hit his senses,
letting him know she wasn't as angry as she let on. Oh, she was a little
upset. There was no doubt about it, but she still wanted him. Now he
just needed to prove to her he hadn't left because he didn't want her just
as badly.

"Glad I'm the first for something," she grumbled.

He tried not to smile at the tone of her jealousy, but damn, she was
so fucking cute and sexy all rolled into one perfect mate. "You'll be the
first and last for many things, Joni," he assured her, letting her hear the
honesty in his words.

"You can put me down now." Joni squirmed in his arms.

"I like you right where you are." He let her slide down his body
even though it was the last thing he wanted, her slight frame making
his much larger one shiver. "See, that was a first. I've never felt that for
a female, ever."

Joni turned away from him, marching across the open space. With
her back to him, he could see her stiffen. "What was a first, besides the
kidnapping thing?"

"I've never felt like that from just holding a female. Dammit, Joni,
look at me," he ordered. When she didn't, he took two steps toward her.

"Don't, Atlas, give me a second to collect my thoughts. I can't think
with you...so close." She held up her hand, her back still to him.

"Why?" he asked.

"What do you mean?" she asked, turning to face him.

"Why do you need a second? Why do you want me to stay away?"
He knew the last was said with more growl than not, but fuck, he'd
spent too long without her.

"You didn't seem to have any problem leaving me after we spent
weeks dancing around one another. I all but threw myself at you when

we were together. You knew I...I had feelings for you, but all the sudden, you were gone, and I was left with this big hole in my life. Once again, Joni was left with nobody to care for her. I was on the outside looking in while everybody else found their other half. I'm done being a—second class citizen. I'll be damned if I'm your dirty little secret. I get it. You're the big bad bear who can't have some fucking female wolf shifter who can't even shift anymore."

Atlas watched as twin tears rolled down her cheeks. He couldn't stand there and allow her to think he didn't care. Screw her needing or wanting space, his bear was ready to tear things apart if he didn't have her in his arms again. "That's not how it was, if you would let me explain," he murmured once he was close enough to hold her.

Like a wild animal, she beat at his chest. Atlas let her hit him, let her yell until he felt her calm, or run out of energy. Either way, he held her until she couldn't stand on her own. "Can I speak now, Konese'?" he asked as he settled them on the sofa in the living area, ignoring the creaking of the furniture underneath him.

"If you break Hollis's and Annie's couch your gonna pay to replace it." She rubbed her face against his plaid shirt, her tears wetting the material.

"I'll replace anything I break." He ran his fingers through her hair, lifting the long locks up to his nose, inhaling her unique scent.

She tried to push away from him. "Stop trying to move out of my arms, woman."

"Some things you break can't be fixed, Atlas," she snarled.

He leaned back so that he could see her face. "Goddess, you're beautiful, Konese'."

"What does that mean?" She blinked up at him.

"Beautiful in Mohican. My clan have strong roots from the Mohicans." He bent and pressed a kiss to her forehead.

"Like Last of the Mohicans?" she asked.

"The telling of the story is like many things, not quite true. Do you truly think that three men and two women, one disguised as a bear, could truly do so much if one wasn't truly a bear? And do you think that they would allow the capture of their female, without punishment? In times such as those, it would've been best to let them think they'd been killed, succumbing to death on a cliff, allowing them the ability to mourn through human funerals, do you not agree?" Atlas continued to run his hand up and down her back, feeling the tension leave her slight frame.

"So, you're saying the history books are wrong?" she asked.

He shrugged. "I'm saying that it's possible the situation wasn't quite the way it was presented."

She huffed. "Why are we even talking about this?"

"You brought it up, Konose," he reminded her.

"That's right. Like I said, you can't fix everything you break with your big bear ass. Let me go." She took a deep breath.

"Tell me what I broke that I can't fix. We'll start there and work my way up, but there's no chance in hell I'm letting you go, ever again. You're my truemate, and you know it. You can feel it, just as I can. Why're you fighting us?" Her anger was making his bear rake at him.

"Seriously? Atlas, you're clearly an alpha. I'm not even a real wolf, not anymore."

He gave her a slight shake, careful of his strength. "Listen to me, little one. Even if you were fully human, you're mine. I don't give two shits about your abilities. I only know you're mine."

Joni rolled her eyes. "Oh, you wanted me so much you couldn't run so fast and far away from me as soon as I told you I cared about you." She bit her lip to stop the words *I loved you* from falling from her mouth.

"Woman, I left because my alpha's mate called me back. She had a half baked scheme cooked up, and I knew if I'd brought you back with me before I took up the role of alpha, she'd have either killed you outright or ordered you killed. I had to follow certain rules. Things are different amongst my clan. I'm not just a grizzly bear, Joni. I—I'm a white bear, and not like a Kermode white bear, but a dire bear. Do you know what that means?"

She leaned away from him, or as far as his arms would let her, shaking her head.

"In the White Bear Clan, it's prophesized that a White Bear is to lead the clan into the future. Before my father, there hadn't been a white bear for hundreds of years. My brothers, Atika and Abyle are twins, yet they aren't white. When I was born a white cub, my father lost his mind, or maybe he'd always been a little unhinged. His bear began turning from pure white to a cream, which the clan said meant he wasn't the true prophesized leader. My bear, on the other hand is snowy white, and well, I'm much larger than most." He looked away from her.

Joni had a feeling he wasn't telling her the complete truth, yet she couldn't sense a lie. "What aren't you telling me, Atlas?"

He fell back against the cushions, letting out a deep breath. "So much, Konese'. Can you trust me when I say nothing I did was ever done without a reason?"

"Why don't you give me the condensed version. I think we both have pasts that aren't really what one would call Hallmark Christmas Card ones, but still, they're ours to tell, right?" She finally looked at the man she couldn't forget, no matter how far she'd run.

"My past is pretty fucking ugly, Joni. You sure you want to hear it? I got more scars inside and out. You think I'm some pretty boy who has it all, but reality is, I'm a fucked up motherfucker who probably doesn't deserve you." He looked away, his bear growling during the last of his words, setting her wolf to pacing inside her.

"I have just as many scars inside me. Trust me. I finally had to make the decision to stop letting the asshole who stole years of my life, years I'll never get back, have the power to continue to do so. If I continued to cower and be a victim, his punishments would continue, but for me, I decided that even though he was dead, I could punish him by trying to be happy, trying to...to move forward with my life, to do all the things he'd denied me. Because do you know what I did for years, what he'd loved to know I did? I felt sorry for myself. It fueled him, gave him power over me, even when he wasn't inflicting pain on me. When I came here, even months after his death, I still held onto the past, reliving the things he'd done, the mental abuse that was as painful as the physical ones he'd made Taryn go through. I allowed him to steal more of me, more of my life. He doesn't deserve a single second more of me or my life. I deserve to be happy. I realized when I came here, when Hollis and Annie let me be a part, even on the outer edges of their Crew, that I deserved to move on with my life, even if it's alone." For the first time in her twenty-five years, she truly felt like she was worth more.

"I want to find whoever that motherfucker was and kill him with my bare hands," Atlas said in a low voice.

Shivers went through her at his low tone. "He's already dead and gone, or I'd actually let you at him. Now, how about you tell me about why you think you're not worthy?"

Joni listened as he recounted his childhood, her eyes widened, tears she tried to keep at bay flowed freely as he spoke of the little boy who only wanted to be loved, but was beaten and almost killed by parents who were supposed to have loved him. "So, you see, I'm not sure how to love someone, but I promise to protect you with every fiber of my being." He said when he finished.

She turned so that she straddled him, placing both palms on his cheeks. "Of course, you know how to love. Look at how you protected your family, how you protected your clan all these years. Goddess, we're a pair." She put her forehead on his. "We can learn to love together, you think?"

"I know the things I feel for you I've never felt for anyone. I know I'll kill anyone who hurts one hair on your head. I know my bear wants to claim you, and so do I, and I know I want to wake up next to you for the rest of my days," he breathed close to her lips.

Joni licked her lips. "I want those things with you, too. What about your clan? I thought they wouldn't accept you mating a wolf. I thought it was like forbidden or something?"

He nibbled her upper lip before answering. "I'm the alpha. I make the rules. Now kiss me before I go crazy, Konese," he ordered.

"Bossy bear," she whispered.

The couch creaked as he shifted them, placing her beneath him. "I'm so much more than bossy, love. Goddess, I've wanted you under me for so long," he muttered. "Tell me you want this."

Joni stared up at Atlas, knowing what he was asking. "Are you asking if I want to make love to you or if you can claim me?"

"Both," he answered.

She looked toward the door, then to the bed not far from them. "I'm thinking the bed would be a better place." She didn't want to mention that this would be a first for her.

Atlas inhaled. "What are you keeping from me?"

She squeezed her eyes shut. "Bossy bear, do you have like superman powers or what?"

His chuckle made her open her eyes. "I guess I'm a little more in tune to you than normal. Now, tell me," he ordered softly.

"I've never...you know, done this." She waved between them. The scant inches he allowed between their chests, not giving her much room to move, had her slapping his chest with the back of her hand.

"Ah, a first for the both of us then." He stood, leaned down, and scooped her into his arms. "I don't think that couch would've handled what I had planned anyhow," he joked.

Joni narrowed her eyes. "Are you trying to tell me you're a virgin? Because let me tell you, I'm not buying what you're selling, bossy bear."

Atlas stumbled. "Goddess no. Wait, don't try to jump out of my arms, dammit. No other female before you even comes to my mind. What I mean is, I've never claimed a female, never wanted to. I'm thirty-three years old. I wish I could say I've never been with anyone else; fuck I wish I could go back in time and not have...but then who knows how that would affect today. All I know is that I'm here with you, right where I'm supposed to be. Goddess willing, I'll be with you everyday for the rest of our lives."

"That sounds good, but who's to say that after you do the deed that you won't run again?" Everyone she's ever cared about found it really easy to leave her when they found something or someone better. Fine, if she was being fair, Taryn and Sky found their truemates, which if she were in their shoes, she'd have done the same. They also had no clue what she'd bargained with Keith all those years ago. She had no plans to tell them either.

"Even if you don't let me claim you, I still plan to convince you, however long it takes. If that means staying here in Wolfs Run with a menagerie of shifters, then so be it." He stopped next to her bed, still holding Joni securely in his arms.

"What about sex—with me I mean?" she stammered.

Atlas smiled. "No sex before you agree to let me claim you. I want it all. The whole shebang. You're my truemate. You know it and I know it. My bear is raking at me, calling me all kinds of a fool, but until you're ready, he and I will just have to live with blue balls." He settled her on the bed, climbing in next to her.

Joni was shocked when he pulled her back into his arms. "What're you doing?"

"Just because there's not going to be a claiming doesn't mean I'm not going to hold you, and stuff," he teased, his fingers trailed down her arm and back up."

His touch sent shivers down her body, awakening parts of her she'd thought had gone dormant. "Hollis isn't going to allow you to...to sleep here."

Atlas snorted. "Hollis may be the alpha here, but I out alpha him every day and night. Now, let's get to know each other again. Tell me what you've been doing since you left Mystic."

Joni growled. "You're really going to do this?"

"Yep," he answered.

Atlas couldn't believe how fun it was teasing Joni. Although his cock didn't agree, his heart was lighter just having her in his arms.

"I've been training and working at the gas station Hollis and Annie own. It's right off the interstate." She bit her lip. "Do you think it was safe to leave them with Lula?"

He rolled to the side, looking down on Joni. "They're safe as long as they tell the truth. Lula and I just met, but I got the feeling she was—a straight shooter."

Joni grabbed the finger he was using to trace her lips, nibbling on the tip. "A straight shooter alright. She can shoot fire out of her mouth for crying out loud."

"Well, if all is on the up and up with them, they'll be fine. I, however, may expire from blue balls, but you don't hear me complaining, do you?" He nudged her thigh with what was obviously his dick, or a pole he'd shoved into his pants.

Feeling a wee bit adventurous and a lot horny herself, she let her hand slip between them, tracing the evidence of his arousal. "Poor, bossy bear, do you need a little help with this?"

"Achwahnaja, I need help with many things, but unless you plan to get naked with me, that will have to wait." His hand covered hers, stilling her movements.

"Hold up, what's that mean, Achwahnaja?" She tried to move her hand, amazed at the length of his cock. "By the way, bossy bear, that thing is huge, like no way in all of Texas is it going to fit inside my vagi-na, huge."

He opened his mouth to answer but closed it.

Chapter Ten

Lula looked at the alpha of the Wilde Crew, liking the name of the shifters that made up the band of misfits that Hollis and his mate had collected. Her eyes shifted to Annie. Some folks thought she spoke oddly, mixing up her words, but Lula was over a millennium, and then some old. A female didn't really divulge her age...that was just rude. She'd studied every culture on every planet, in every realm, popping in every decade or century, depending on her boredom. Dragons got bored easily, such was the long life of theirs. She flicked her fingers, sending both Hollis and the possible treacherous Annie moving into chairs like little ragdolls, only she did it nicely, almost gently. "Ah, much better. Don't you feel better getting off your feet since you both have worked all day?" she asked innocently. "Ps. You're welcome." She lifted her tulle skirt out and did a small curtsy.

Hollis growled. "What the hell are you?" He tried to stand but couldn't.

"For the moment, I'm a friend, luckily for you," Lula answered him, walking around the large kitchen, picking up knickknacks. "You've created a very nice place here, Alpha. How long have you two been together?"

"Why don't you get to the point of this...whatever it is?" he ordered.

Lula turned, a small figure in her hand. "Why don't we ask your mate who she's been in contact with in the last twenty-four hours, instead." Lula pulled a chair in front of Annie, turning to straddle it backward, her arms hanging over the top of it. "Wow, this isn't as easy as the guys make it look." She got back up and spun it, so she sat on it the correct way. "Much better. Now, let's try it again. Want to tell your mate who you spoke with about your friend out in the barn?" She tossed the figure in the air, catching it in her hand, then did it again. "This is so cute, so delicate. Who made it?"

113

Hollis growled. "One of my boys."

Lula placed it on the table. "He's very good. It's very lifelike. Do you like wolves, Annie?"

The female swallowed but nodded. "I like all my, our, crew."

"Then why did you betray Joni?" Lula picked the wolf figure back up, turning it to face Annie.

"I—I didn't. I swear, there was a message on The Lost Ones board that only other shifters know about. It's what we use for shifters who need a place to go. I received an email from a concerned mother. This person claimed she was the mother who was missing her daughter. I swear I only wanted to help Joni. I thought if I knew more," Annie swallowed. "I thought I could help fix her," she cried.

Lula tapped the table. "What did you tell this concerned female?"

Annie shook her head. "Nothing. I mean, she asked where her daughter was, threatened extreme retribution if I didn't give her our location, but something didn't ring true. She wouldn't answer my questions about what was wrong with her, only demanded to know where we were located. I told her I'd have her daughter get in contact with her. I haven't heard from her since."

Hollis growled, his anger beating at Lula but her dragon was the dominate in the room.

Lula leaned forward, ignoring Hollis and his alpha growl to *stop*. Silly men and their thought to stop her. She placed one finger on Annie's forehead, searching through the lioness's memory, seeing for herself the truth of what she'd said. Oh, she could've done this to begin with, but Lula liked to see if a person would willingly be honest first. It made her next decision easier. "You speak the truth. You actually care for Joni, which is good news. However, the so called concerned mother has had a week since her first contact with you, and from your last conversation a day. Which means, they could be right outside your door at any moment, ready to pounce on your poor unsuspecting booties."

"I would know if they'd entered my territory, female. If you could do that, then why didn't you do it in the first place?" Hollis nearly stood, his anger giving him extra strength as he glared at Lula.

Lula patted his arm. "Easy, coyote. You two would've made beautiful cubities. Hmm, because I'm in the giving mood, I think I'll see what I can do to make that happen. Would you like that?"

Annie turned to look at Hollis, then back at Lula. "We can't have children of our own."

"Pfft, you've never had a dragon on your side. Now, there's trouble on its way, and it's coming here, so you'll need to rally your crew. I think," she paused and tapped her chin. "Well, I'd say we've got a couple days and a very stubborn wolf in hiding that needs a bossy bear to do his boo thang, so let's put a pin in this discussion. I gots places to go, a goddess to see, a Fey Queen and her babies to nuggle. You know, a dragon's job is just never done. Tootles," Lula said before she stood up, and then because she felt like fucking with the couple, clicked her heels three times. "I want to go home." She grinned at their shocked expressions. "Just kidding." Then she disappeared, pulling her power from them as she went.

Atlas felt the shift in the air. "Your friends are safe from Lula." Goddess, he breathed a sigh of relief. The female was one of the only beings on Earth who actually scared the shit out of him, which was saying a lot since he hadn't been scared of much since he'd been a cub.

"Do you know what she is?" Joni asked.

He nodded. "Can we talk about something else now?"

She licked her bottom lip. "Like what? Like how you left me, or how you showed up out of the blue with a crazy pink haired dragon female?"

Atlas didn't like where her mind was going, or her questioning. However, he did like the way her lip was nice and puffy from her biting and the way it looked wet from her tongue. His bear wanted a taste, or maybe that was him who wanted it. Either way, Atlas was done denying them both. His head lowered, keeping his eyes locked onto her bright green ones, letting her see his intent. If she didn't want his kiss, she could turn her head. Of course, he'd follow, but when his lips touched hers, she sighed into his mouth, opening for him.

He swept inside, taking the kiss deeper, licking over her teeth, then swept the roof of her mouth, wanting to memorize her taste. "Goddess, it's been too long since I've tasted you. Like berries and mint." He sealed his lips over hers, not letting her respond. If she shut him down again, he was sure his bear would need to go out and hunt. Hell, in fucking Texas cornfields, Atlas didn't think there was a prey big enough to satisfy his bear.

The sweet smell of her arousal permeated the air around them. Mothereffingsonofabitch, he didn't know how he was going to stop, but damn, he promised her he would. "You're delicious, you know that, right?" he murmured, trailing biting kisses down her neck to where her shoulder was exposed. He nipped the area he wanted to mark, watching the skin form little goosebumps.

"You didn't answer me earlier," she gasped, arching her back.

Atlas bit one hardened nub through her shirt. His Joni was far from small breasted. Hell, she was downright curvy and perfect for him in every single way. At six feet seven and over two hundred and seventy-five pounds, he needed a woman who would fit his palms. Joni, while not big, was at least five seven, with breasts that filled his palms and an ass that would be more than enough for him to hold while he held her against him. Damn, the image of her legs wrapped around his hips, his hands holding her ass while he pumped in and out of her had his cock jerking. "What was your question?" he asked, coughing to clear his throat.

"You called me a name again. What did it mean? Oh, good goddess, what are you doing to me?"

Atlas took the other distended nipple into his mouth while he plucked the one he'd just had between his fingers. How he wished the two layers of fabric didn't separate them. "Achwahnaja means love," he answered.

Joni grabbed the back of his head, tugging on his hair. "You called me love. Do you think you love me, Atlas?"

He stilled. "Love is a fairytale, Joni. I care about you. I'll take care of you for all our lives. I'll be the best mate, the best father to our children, and I'll protect you with my life. As for love, what is love but a word that's thrown around for humans to excuse the way they act. For us, our kind, a truemate is the Fates way of ensuring we are with the ones that we're fated to be with. That's stronger than any word the humans have come up with. I know the thought of never seeing you, of never hearing your voice, or seeing you hurt brings me to my knees. If that's what humans call love, then we can call it that. You're who my bear calls his. You're who I want to spend the rest of my time on this Earth with. I don't have flowery words; they are just words. I can give you me, all of me. Is that enough for you, Achwahnaja?"

Atlas lifted up enough to see her reaction. If she denied him because he couldn't love her, couldn't give her the words she needed to hear, he wasn't sure what he'd do. He was damaged by his past.

"Silly bear, of course you're enough for me. Now, shut up and kiss me and show me what the fuss of making love is all about. Also, this shirt is all wet now, can you take it off me, please?" She wiggled her arms up and over her head.

He growled, looking at her with her arms over her head, green eyes sparkling with mischief. "If we do this, I might not be able to stop," he warned.

"Promises, promises, bossy bear. Come on, less talky, more action. There wasn't anything I could think of that rhymed with talky other than walky, and well, I don't want you walking." She wiggled again.

Atlas's eyes went to the twin globes jiggling as she moved. "One day, I'll fuck these, too."

"Oh, that sounds dirty, bossy bear."

He growled. "You keep calling me bossy bear, and I'll show you just how bossy I can be."

Her eyes heated. Oh, his little female liked the idea. He couldn't wait to get her back to his home and see just how far he could go with being her bossy bear.

Joni reached down with both hands, ripping her shirt over her head. "You're way too slow, slow bear. How about that name?"

Atlas's bear rumbled, wanting to show a little dominance to their soon to be truemate. "You like this bra, Achwahnaja?"

Joni nodded. "It's hard to find bras that fit these double D's," she explained.

"Take it off then," he ordered, sitting back on his heels as he straddled her thighs.

She flicked the catch in the middle, slowly moving the cup on the right while leaving the left breast covered. "I might need to sit up to take it off properly."

He helped her sit up, shifting their legs so that he was between her thighs, taking over the removal for her, ripping his own shirt off while he had her so close to him. They both moaned when he pulled her chest against his. "Damn, you're so soft," he whispered.

"You're not," she sighed, moving back and forth. "Goddess, I think I could come from this alone."

One of his hands slid down, lifting her up, rubbing her covered pussy up and down his jean-covered cock. Never had he been jealous of cloth before, but damned if he didn't want to be a pair of yoga pants right then and there.

"If you're going to come, it's going to be on my fingers, tongue, or cock, not a pair of panties." Atlas pressed her back onto the bed gently, following her down, keeping his weight from crushing her with his elbows on either side of her body. "I can't believe we're here." He shook his head.

Joni brought her hand up, tracing his brows. "Why are you frowning?"

"There's so much I need to tell you."

"Sssh, talk more later. Right now, lets just feel. We've wasted too much time, running from each other."

Joni didn't want to voice her biggest fear, the one that he would reject her once he realized her wolf was really, truly gone for good. For once, she wanted to take what she wanted, and that was one night with the big bad bossy bear. She may not be able to call on her beast and do what she'd been born to do anymore, but she felt the other being more when she was with him. Even now, with him growling above her, her own skin felt more alive, similar to the first time she'd shifted. Goddess, she missed shifting.

"What's wrong?" he asked.

She blinked, pushing thoughts of what couldn't be aside. "I was just thinking if you didn't get to stepping, I might just have to take matters into my own...hands." She maneuvered her hand between them, knowing it would incite Atlas.

"I'll tie those hands to the bedpost, female."

At his words, her inner hussy literally sat up and said, *yes please.* The bits of fabric between her thighs became even wetter as she lifted against him, wanting, needing him to do something.

"Easy, Konese', I got you." Atlas brushed his lips over hers, slowly moving down her body, nipping the bits of flesh he encountered, marking her as his for any who happened to see her. Of course, if anyone saw her unclothed, he'd kill them. Her stomach quivered beneath his kisses. The drawing of his tongue and lips made her abdominal muscles contract. He dipped his tongue into her belly button, watching as the muscles in her abdomen contracted. His little female had gained some strength in not only mind, but body, while she'd been away. Scooting farther down, he used his teeth to tug at the band on her pants, pulling them down with the use of his hands as well.

"Fuck, baby, your scent is driving me crazy, you know that?"

She tried to pull his head away when he stuck his nose between her thighs, still held together by the pants and panties, but Atlas wasn't having any of it. "No," he barked. "I will do with this body what I please. You know why?" He looked up, waiting for her to release her hold on his hair. "Tell me what I want to hear, Konese'."

"Because I'm yours," she whispered.

Atlas nodded. "That's right, and I'm yours. You want to pull my hair, scratch my back, hell claw your name into my skin, you go right ahead. I'll wear your marks with pride, love." He used the word she was used to hearing, not the Mohican word for love, wanting her to know and recognize how he felt.

Her sigh was music to his ears, seconds before she relaxed her hold. Atlas finished pulling her pants and panties off, taking in the first sight of his truemate completely open to him. "Perfect." The one word was a prayer and a thank you in one. He placed a kiss on the top of her mound, then settled back between her splayed thighs, his shoulders opening her up for him. With his left hand, he played with the lips covering paradise, spreading the sweet juice spilling out of her pussy, then spread her open with two fingers. "Damn, you're so fucking pretty, even here. You're little clit is so hard." He licked the tiny little hardened nub, using his right hand on her stomach to hold her in place when she jerked.

"Oh my gawd, what are you doing?"

"Well, if you have to ask, I guess I should do a better job," he said with a wicked tone.

He let his tongue roll around her clit, then licked a slow path down, circling the opening to her pussy, humming at her entrance. Her sweet juices were running down the crack of her ass. Atlas coated one of his fingers in her cream, pressing inside her tight little pussy at the same time he sucked her clit into his mouth. Her scream was followed by the hard pulse and flex of her orgasm. "Damn, that was one. Let's see if we can do that again." He spoke against her soaked flesh, pumping his finger in and out, letting her ride out the orgasm, slowing as he felt her body's pulses stop. He knew just how to bring her back up and again, working her slowly, adding a second finger inside her, using his tongue and fingers. Her body jerked, her moans egging him on.

"Atlas, I...dear goddess, you're killing me. I think I'm going to come again."

He lifted his head, watching as she tossed her head back, her hips lifting into his thrusting fingers. Knowing he needed to stretch her to fit him, he added a third finger, slowly pumping them in and out. "Come on, Konese', come for me."

"You're going to kill me," she moaned.

"I want to make sure everyone knows you're mine. I'm staking an undeniable claim to everyone that you're mine," he said, thrusting his fingers into the heart of her, pressing his tongue over the throbbing distended clit, begging for his attention. With each jerk of her body, he wanted her even more, wanted to hear her call his name.

"Atlas, yes, fuck, I'm coming!" His name burst from her lips as she came again as her sweet orgasm rolled over her, her pleasure filling his mouth.

He surged to his knees, leaning over her, looking into her glassy green eyes. "I want to claim you, every part of you."

"Goddess, yes. Inside me. I need you. No, I want you inside me more than I want my next breath," she panted, her body still shaking, overcome from what he'd done to her.

Keeping her thighs spread with him between them, he shimmied out of his clothes, holding her gaze with his own. "I'll go slow, Achwah-naja," he promised, praying he could actually keep his word. He positioned the head of his cock at her entrance, rubbing along her little slit, coating himself in her juices.

She hummed in approval, the sweet bliss of feeling her body beneath him almost had him slamming inside her. "You're so wet, Joni." He pressed inside an inch. "So tight," he paused, looking down at where they connected, concentrating, then moving forward a little more.

Joni gasped, her body freezing. "I think you're too big."

A bead of sweat tricked down his jaw, landing on her chest. "It's okay, just relax." Fuck, he thought he'd die if he didn't get inside her sooner, rather than later, but didn't want to scare or ruin this first time with his mate. Leaning down, he covered her mouth with his, kissing away her protest, then moved his right hand back down, playing with the little bundle of nerves at the top of her sex, feeling her body relax. Slowly, he worked another inch inside followed by another until he was finally seated fully where he longed to be, their bodies flush together.

He lifted from their kiss, peering down at her, needing to memorize every moment for all eternity. "Goddess, I've never seen a more beautiful sight in my entire life," he swore.

"You're inside me," she whispered, her voice ragged.

Atlas grinned. "That I am. You ready for me to move?" he asked.

She nodded, her inner muscles flexing, almost sending him over the edge.

"Damn, don't do that," he warned, smiling down at her as she did it again. "I see I'm going to have to take you in hand." He began moving in and out, slowly at first then faster, filling her, stamping her with his possession with every slow glide in and out. Sweat dripped off him, landing on her, but instead of revulsion on her face like he'd seen before, she gasped, her hand lifting to rub it into her skin. "Damn, you undo me, Konese." His thrusts picked up, gaining in speed and urgency, her hips meeting his thrust for thrust.

"I'm close, Joni, need you to come with me." Her sweet little pussy gloved him like she'd been made for him, and she had, fitting him perfectly.

"Yes, right there," Joni yelled, swiveling her hips.

He thrust again and again, harder, each one becoming more frantic, driving them both higher. The feel of her claws at his back had him leaning toward her neck, and the cord that he wanted to mark. "Mine," he snarled, biting down, her blood filling his mouth.

Her ankles locked around his back, her hips arched against him, her scream echoing around them.

Chapter Eleven

Joni bucked against Atlas; her orgasm continuing long after he bit her. His *mine* had her wolf rising, the need to claim him greater than anything she'd ever felt in her entire twenty-five years. "Yes, yours," she agreed. Her wolf howled, teeth she hadn't felt burst through her gums, almost painfully. "Mine," she snarled and lunged forward, biting down on the muscle between his shoulder and neck.

Atlas jerked, his cock surging inside her, his hand fisted in her hair holding her to him. "Fuck yes, claim me," he roared.

Joni was sure everyone within a hundred miles could hear her bossy bear as he yelled, but she was helpless to do anything, but do as he said, and then her body took over, orgasming again. She screamed his name around his shoulder, releasing him as she fell back, then leaned up to lick the wound.

Atlas shifted onto his knees, bringing her up to straddle him, keeping them connected, surging deeper, their chests rose and fell together. "You're mine, and I'm yours, forever," he growled, his blue eyes lighter.

Joni nodded, feeling her wolf prowling the surface. "Forever," she agreed, her voice deeper.

"Your wolf wants to shift. Tell her after I finish making love to you."

He began lifting and pulling her back down, his arms doing most of the work as he jackhammered in and out of her. Joni not wanting to stay still, leaned forward, taking his lower lip into her mouth, biting down. Goddess, she had no idea what her action would do to her bossy bear, having him lose all control wasn't it, but she'd be damned if she didn't love it as he began slamming in and out. One hand gripped her hair, the other her ass as he fucked her hard and fast, until they were both coming together, yelling each other's names. There was no doubt she was going to be sore, or that everyone would know what happened, but Joni couldn't help the happy sigh that left her lips.

"Thank you for coming for me," she whispered against his neck by the spot she'd bitten. Her eyes widened at the claiming mark.

His dick twitched. "Always." He lay her backward, slowly pulling out with a groan.

Joni opened her mouth to respond, but agony ripped along her joints. "Atlas, something is wrong." She reached for him.

Atlas sat up. "What is it?"

She shook her head, her body spasming. "I...I don't know. My wolf is howling like she's hurting inside me." She folded her arms around her stomach. "I need to go outside. This doesn't feel right."

The fact her mate was on his feet and had her in his arms before the last word left her mouth showed he was as worried as she was. He had her out the door and down the stairs before she felt a spasm hit her. "What's happening?" she cried.

"Fuck, I don't know." He held her tighter, looking toward the farmhouse, wondering if he should call for the coyote and his mate.

"Put me down, Atlas. I'm...I'm going to shift, but my wolf is scared." She could hear the fear in her voice.

Atlas put her on her feet just as the first pop of bones began, Joni couldn't remember her first shift as a child, could only remember it wasn't all that pleasant. "This isn't—like before." Her teeth ached. Hell, everything hurt. Every bone and muscle felt on fire, her mind scrambled to keep up, then she tried to retreat inside her wolf only to realize even her beast wasn't the same.

Just as she was sure she would rather die than endure any more, the cool feel of grass was beneath her panting wolven body. She felt a warm hand running over her spine, familiar, yet her wolf snarled.

"Easy, Achwahnaja, it's me, Atlas." A deep voice called.

Joni lifted her head off one paw, turning to look up at the human male, alarmed to see tears flowing from him. She whined, realizing in her wolf form she couldn't talk.

"It's going to be fine, baby. Just rest. We'll figure it out," he promised.

She didn't understand what he was talking about. It had been so long since she'd shifted it had taken a lot out of her, which was why it had hurt and why she was so exhausted. She looked down at the ground. A large white paw crossed over another had her scrambling backward. In her haste to get away, she knocked Atlas on his ass. Hearing him curse, she twisted to check on him, her head looming over him. *Holy shit, what the hell is going on?*

"Joni, I need you to stay calm. My bear is a dire white bear, remember?" Atlas spoke inside her mind.

She stared down at her mate, his voice easing some of her fears. She'd never had a connection as clear as what she felt with Atlas, not even when her old alpha had tortured her. The last had Atlas growling in her head. *"What does that mean?"* she asked trying to distract Atlas.

"I'm putting a pin in that little tidbit of info for later. As for what a dire means for you and me...I suspect it means you as my truemate, have now become a dire white wolf. At least by the looks of you. Fuck, you're gorgeous, Achwahnaja." He placed both hands behind her ears and rubbed.

"I've never heard of a dire anything before except in a situation which means really bad. Can I shift back? I don't feel like I'm in control, here." True worry engulfed her. Unlike her wolf before, this one seemed more in control of her.

Atlas kissed the tip of her nose, making Joni growl. *"I can alpha order you both to shift, but I think she needs to run. You've both gone a long time without shifting. The only problem is, I'm not sure what there is for prey around here. I don't want you or I eating something that's not...on the approved menu."*

"Can you reach out to Hollis and ask him? I'd hate to do anything that would hurt him or his crew." Goddess, she sounded like a little whiner ass baby, and her wolf didn't like it. *Too bad, I'm the alpha here,* she thought, taking back a little control.

"Good girl, you need to assert yourself with your beast from the very beginning, or she'll be harder to control." Atlas closed his eyes.

Atlas kept a hand on Joni's huge ass white wolf, loving the softness of her fur. Damn, he had no clue mating with him would change her from a regular wolf to a white wolf, let alone dire wolf. Using his alpha powers, he called out to Hollis. *"Hollis, is there any parameters you have for us hunting?"*

"I'm assuming you're not talking on two legs?" Hollis answered back.

"Ah no, and there's not just a wolf and bear, but two dires gonna be hunting," he said, waiting with bated breath.

"How the hell did that happen?" Hollis growled through their link.

"Oh, what do we have here?"

Atlas growled at the sound of Lula's voice. "Female, don't you have any self-preservation inside that pink head of yours?"

Lula tilted her head to the side. "My head is not pink, big bear. Now, let me see this pretty girl. Aren't you a pretty girl? Oh yes you are. Yes, you are. Come here, let Lula pet you," Lula cooed.

Joni growled; the sound sent shivers down Atlas's spine. *"That female is getting on my nerves."*

Atlas kept his hand firmly on the top of her head. *"Don't, she's a dragon, I think she out sizes us."*

"Very wise, big bear. I'm much larger than both of you combined, but she's very impressive. Look how the moon shines on her coat. Now, who wants to go play fetch on Fey, hmm?" Lula clapped.

Joni tilted her head to the side. *"Is she crazy?"*

"*It's rude to talk inside your head to him and think I can't hear, big wolf,*" Lula chastised.

"Hey, that's not nice either." Joni swatted at Lula, making the other female jump backward but Lula laughed.

"Oh, I forgot she's got that whole human thing going on and hates to be called big," Lula huffed. "Silly females. Now, come along, there's hunting to be done. Big bear, you coming or what?"

Atlas gripped Joni by the fur near her nape. "You sure we'll be safe in Fey?" His first and last duty was to protect his mate.

Purple eyes met his over Joni's head. "While my Queen is busy with her mates and babies, my duty is to take care of her people. She," Lula pointed at Joni before continuing, "is her people and since you are her mate, you are now my people to take care of. Now, shift before we go, since I'm not sure how you'll do on Fey. Word of warning, big bear," Lula waited a beat. "I tell you what you can and can't eat. You both will listen to me as your leader, alpha or no." The last was said with more authority than Atlas had ever uttered.

He nodded. "Joni, I'm going to change, but I wanted to warn you and your wolf to be prepared...I'm not a regular grizzly."

"We're aware and ready to see our mate," Joni rumbled. Their link was getting stronger with each passing second.

Atlas took a deep breath, then moved away from both females. His bear was as familiar to him as the man. With a thought, he shifted, becoming the white dire bear. Instead of needing to hunt, his bear walked up to its mate, nudging her side. Joni tilted her neck, showing him the mating mark even her shift couldn't hide. A growl escaped his huge mouth as he licked the spot, then he met the amused smirk of the pink haired pixie.

"You two ready, or you need a minute to boink?" Lula asked.

Atlas lifted a lip to snarl. *"We're ready, female,"* he said through the link she'd opened earlier.

Lula clapped, then placed a hand on Joni first before calling to Atlas. "Come here, big bear. By the way, I'm told the trip through realms can be a little sickening to some of those not used to traveling in such a way. However, I've never had a problem with any of my passengers. I hope you both are like my others." With those words, she gave a tug.

Atlas reached out to Joni, needing to be connected to her as well. The ground beneath them disappeared at a rate he was sure had his stomach turning inside out. *I'm with you,* he assured his mate through their link, fighting to not be Lula's first upchucker.

Joni blinked the world into focus, trying to orient herself once Lula sat them on their feet, or rather paws. She still couldn't believe she was a huge white wolf. No, a dire wolf. She'd been outcast from her friends and family before for what she couldn't do, now she truly wouldn't be welcomed back. The thought had her snarling.

"Oh, look, our puppy has huge fangs," Lula said.

"Yes, what better to eat you with," Joni snarled, shocking herself when the words came out of her wolf. "What the hell?"

Lula skipped around. "Here on Fey, many things are possible, like you being able to talk in whatever form you take. Now, what should we do, and please don't say boink your mate? My sensitive dragon ears and eyes can't handle things of that nature. Besides, those who do the boinking here, tend to get pregnant with entire baseball teams. You ready to batter up, big bear?"

Looking over at her mate she took in his slightly off color and feared something was wrong. "Atlas, are you okay?" Shoot, had traveling wherever they had damaged him like Lula said?

"Baseball teams? Like, several cubs?" he asked.

Joni pounced, knocking the big bear over until they were rolling down a grassy hill unlike any she'd seen on Earth. "Seriously? You had me scared your organs were outside your body, or your brain was left on...some other world." She bit his shoulder where her mark was.

His happy laughter lifted his huge bear belly, knocking her off of him. "If my organs were on the outside, wouldn't you see them?"

Lula made a gagging sound. "First off, that would be totally gross unless I was hungry, then pass me the yum yum sauce. Second, are you two done rolling around like children? I brought you here to hunt, not do that?"

By that, Joni assumed she meant not bat paws at each other, but damn, her mate was truly magnificent with his shiny white coat and light blue eyes.

"I'm glad you think I'm perfect." Atlas stood on his hind legs, turning in a full circle.

"Oh, lord love a duckling, palease. I will turn you into a monkey if you don't go chase a cat or something."

"I think the saying is love a duck, but let's not split hairs. I feel the urge to run and hunt. Not sure about actually eating anything, though." Even when Keith had been in charge, she'd not wanted to partake in the taking down of a live animal. Goddess, was she a vegan wolf?

"Your inner thoughts are quite fascinating, big wolf. However, I don't want you trying to split my hairs. You really do think and say weird things." Lula plopped down on the grass, which appeared to look more turquoise than green. "Now, here's your only real rules. One," Lula took a breath, squinting up at the sky. "Don't eat anything that looks like a person. Two, don't talk to strangers, so basically only talk to each other or me or Jenna. Three, you best get going, the clock is tick tocking." Lula lay on her back. "Oh, and four, if I holler, come a runnin' 'cause shits going down."

Joni looked at the female lying as if she hadn't a care in the world. "We do have permission to be here, yes?"

Lula waved a hand in the air, her feet pointing towards the dual suns. "Of course, I mean, we're here, duh."

"Lula, are we going to be eaten by a huge ass dragon, or no?" Atlas growled, coming to stand over Lula, his white bear on all fours.

With her eyes squinting up at him, which didn't make Joni happy, the dragon waved again. "The only dragons here are me and my mama. If you see a big angry dragon, you best shift to human and cry for Jenna, or me. Now, bye, I'm trying to nap." Lula closed her eyes, letting out a loud snore.

"Come on, she wouldn't have brought us here if we weren't allowed. Let's just let our beasts run. I feel the need to let off some steam," Atlas said nudging Joni in the side.

Joni gave one last look toward the weird female, then turned away, the strangeness of their surroundings forgotten as she gave herself over to the wolf.

Chapter Twelve

Atlas let Joni lead, watching her back while they ran. The species of animals on the realm Lula had taken them to a lot different than what he'd encountered on Earth. His bear scented prey within minutes of their run, but he didn't track it, instead kept pace with Joni, allowing her to lead.

"Are you hungry, bossy bear?" she asked through their link. The voice of her wolf was slightly different than her human one, which had his bear going still.

"I am, but I'm content to give you space until you find your footing." He nudged her side when he felt a predator growing ever closer. Not that he didn't think he couldn't take it, but he didn't want to spoil his time with his mate.

Her laughter floated into his mind. *"Ah, I think I am ready to leap with you. Which way?"*

The sound of rushing water gave him an idea as well as the perfect direction to take them. His bear moved in front of the huge wolf, rubbing against her as he passed. He was running so fast, he nearly jumped off the edge of the hill, falling into what was probably a deep lake.

"Holy shit, that was close." Joni skidded to a halt next to him, dirt and grass flying up as her paws dug into the ground to halt her momentum.

"You ain't kidding." He looked down at the drop and then back at the wolf. "Can you swim, Konese'?" The sound of the rushing water came from a huge waterfall, which Atlas was sure would be an easy trek in their shifted form, but would be a lot more fun in their human ones. He still couldn't wrap his head around their ability to talk and understand one another while they were in their animal forms. Hell, it would be their luck they'd be unable to communicate as humans.

"Yes, what do you have in mind?"

He showed her through their link, feeling her trepidation at what could be below the surface. "How do we know the loch ness monster ain't down there ready to eat our tasty asses?"

Atlas huffed. "You taste amazing, but my big hairy ass would cause it indigestion. Besides, I don't sense a predator." His animal would sense a threat.

Her wolf nudged his shoulder. "Fine, but if I get eaten, I'm coming back to haunt you."

Atlas huffed, his form of a laugh as a bear, then turned to lead the way down toward the falling water. The closer they got, the louder the water became.

"The only thing that'll be eating you will be me," he promised.

Sweet arousal filled the air, making Atlas wish they were in their human forms. Lula's warning about fucking and creating multiple little Joni's had his bear hurrying forward.

"I can totally see where your mind just went, crazy bear, and the answer is hell naw. I am not having one, let alone a slew of little pupperbears, or direwolbears. Heck, what would we have, anyhow?" She tried to picture what their combination would be but came up completely blank.

"Trust me, the Goddess wouldn't give us anything we couldn't handle," Atlas assured her.

"Yeah, but we're dealing with two different Goddesses here. Yours and mine. How do we know they play nice together?" Joni brushed against his side.

Atlas ducked under the rushing water, finding what he had been sure he'd find, a hidden little alcove just big enough for him and Joni, or a dragon. He opened his senses, searching for any form of life. "Nothing has been back here for some time. I think we're safe to shift if we want."

Joni shook her head. "I thought you needed to shift. Hell, usually after a shift I'd...or rather my wolf would, but something about being here has calmed us." She lay on her stomach, her head resting on her front paws.

He stared down at the miracle that was his mate. "I'm glad Lula brought us here. Being a dire has been different than a normal grizzly. I have never had anyone to share my world with." He turned away from Joni, walking closer to the edge to peer out at the water below.

"Do you want to go for a swim?" Joni asked.

Atlas turned to stare down at her, surprised she'd been able to move without him hearing her. Of course, he'd been busy thinking or so relaxed he'd not been paying attention.

"I'd be offended if I were a lesser female." She too looked down at the colorful water. "It's strange to look at water that isn't blue or green, or even muddy brown, but a pretty pink and purple," she remarked.

"I wonder if it's saltwater or fresh?" Atlas reached out to Lula, not wanting to risk Joni being injured if they jumped in for a swim in either form.

"*The water is fine for you to frolic in no matter what form you take. Word of warning though, don't eat anything that talks to you.*" Lula's swift response gave him pause.

"Does she mean there's like mermaids or talking fish?" Joni questioned.

Atlas looked down into the water. "Hell, with her and this realm, it's hard to say. You ready to jump and see?"

Joni nodded her wolven head. "Let's go in like this. If there's a mermaid, I'd rather be a dire wolf than a human."

With a swipe of her tongue, Joni gave a growl, then leapt into the water first, the long drop clearly not causing his mate any fear. No way was he going to be a scaredy bear, he leapt as well, barely keeping the wussy scream from escaping. When his bear hit the warm water, he quickly began swimming toward the surface, searching for Joni. The radiant sparkle in her green eyes brought the same to his as he spotted her treading water in her human form. "Damn, you're gorgeous," he rumbled, shifting with a thought into human as well.

"Remember don't sexy wexy, bossy bear. As much as I loved having you inside me, there is no way I want a league of bossy baby wolfiebears." She splashed water toward him.

He swam toward her. "There are other things we can do that doesn't have me penetrating your lady box." His lips turned up in a grin at her very unladylike snort.

"Excuse me, but where the hell did you come up with that...that term for my magical vagina?" She floated on her back, staring up at the sky. "Did you notice there are two suns?"

Atlas copied her pose, floating on his back, too. "I did. Strange, but I bet when they visit Earth, or other realms they find the differences weird as well. Do you burn easily?" Her skin was almost porcelain in color, yet he didn't see any sign of a freckle.

Joni's arms moved back and forth, keeping her afloat. "I don't think so. I've never done so in the past. Do you feel any heat beating down on you? Wouldn't there be that if I was going to burn?" She lifted one arm up, twisting it back and forth.

"Pardon me, but what in the actual fuck are you two naked humanish people doing?"

Atlas surged forward, putting Joni behind him, facing the female dragon. "My name is Atlas, and this is my mate Joni. Our friend Lula brought us here."

A huff of smoke met his announcement.

"If you give us a moment, we will call our friend and be out of your...space." Hell, he didn't know what to call where they were, only knew he was in a vulnerable position as the dragon stood on the opposite side of the waterfall from where they'd entered and was twice as big as Lula.

"I will call my daughter. You two humans come on out of there. I think you've scared the locals enough already," she huffed again.

His need to shift into his bear was strong, but one look at the female let him know she could literally squish them both like bugs without even lifting a foot. Nope, all she'd have to do was twitch her tail, or shoot a flame from her mouth, and he was sure they'd both be burned to a crisp.

"Very wise, my bear friend. If I'm not mistaken, there's my recalcitrant daughter now," Belle said, looking up at the sky.

Atlas and Joni swam toward the side, he helped her climb up just as Lula landed, magic swirled around them, clothing both of them in jeans and T-shirts. He nodded toward the smaller dragon.

"Mother, what are you doing here?" Lula asked, her voice higher than Atlas had ever heard.

"Really, Lula, that's what you ask me?" Belle flicked her finger toward the two humans. "What're they doing here? Is Jenna aware you brought a beast of another Goddess to her realm?"

Lula ducked her head, her tail swishing back and forth. "Well, you see, he's mated to one of hers, therefore he's now one of Jenna's, and they needed a place to go because they're not normal shifters. Hence, here." She waved her wing, nearly whacking Atlas and Joni over in the process. "Woops, my bad," she said as she tucked her wings back in close to her shimmering pink body.

Belle paced away from them. "Let me think for a moment."

"Sssh, this could take a minute, my mother isn't much of a thinker, she's more of a doer, and by that I mean she usually just kills." Lula spoke out of the side of her mouth loud enough Atlas was sure everyone in the realm had heard her.

"Lula, I will put you over my knee, child," her mother warned.

Atlas would've laughed at the sight of the huge pink dragon pretending to zip her lip as the even bigger dragon threatened to spank her daughter, but even he as a dire, was tiny in comparison to them. Nope, he just wanted to make it back to Earth with his mate, and all his limbs in working order.

"Alright, we need to get them back to Earth. Nothing has disturbed the Goddesses as of yet, right? Like, they've not created offspring here, tying this realm to them. They've not killed any of our kind, so they don't owe our Goddess." Belle nodded. "Take them to Earth, it's a neutral zone. I can sense they're truemates, which means the Goddesses have agreed for their mating to be possible. Lula, you—" Belle's words were cut off as quiet fell over the meadow.

"Ah, I see our children have found their way to your realm," an ethereal voice spoke.

Lula and Belle fell to their knees, looking behind Atlas and Joni.

"Kneel, you two," Lula ordered.

Atlas turned to see who'd spoken with such a beautiful voice, making his bear hum inside his body.

Joni felt her wolf whimper. "Yes, although I didn't realize they'd cause such a stir. I guess my dragon guardian is a little overprotective. Thank you, Belle, you've done very well. Lula, I appreciate you taking such good care of these two. Can we see you two in your shift?"

This time, her wolf did a good imitation of a purr at the female's request. Joni felt the beast inside her pressing forward. Her hand reached for Atlas's. "Shift with me?" she asked.

"Always," he agreed.

"I think you should step a few paces away if you'll get as big as I think you will," the first female said.

Her wolf didn't whimper this time. Joni nodded, allowing Atlas to release her hand and move away far enough to allow room for both their dire animals to grow. Her body began to shift, faster than ever, only she felt no pain, no popping of bones, or stretching of skin as she became the huge white wolf.

She looked down at the odd colored grass through her wolven eyes, marveling at the white paws that would be larger than a human head. "I could literally palm a basketball with these things," she said, marveling again at the ease it was to speak in her wolven form.

"This realm as well as mine, gives you the ability as that is your natural form here. You both are just as beautiful as I'd imagined."

Joni looked at the Goddess she'd worshipped but never thought she'd meet, gasping at the almost too beautiful female before her. "What do I call you?"

"Goddess is fine. Your journey is not complete yet, little one. Belle, do not be angry at Lula, for she wouldn't have been able to bring Atlas here if it wasn't my wish, or hers." The Goddess nodded toward the other female.

"Thank you, Goddess," Atlas whispered.

Joni noticed he hadn't taken his eyes off of the Goddess his bear worshipped. She waited for jealousy to hit, but only felt love and acceptance.

"As it should, female," the Goddess spoke.

Joni swung her head in the direction of the voice. "Are you reading my thoughts?"

Both Goddesses smiled. "There are no secrets from us. We are the original creators of all of you. No, we don't see and or hear everything, but if you are in our presence, there is nothing you say, or do, we do not know. Past, present, or future. Now, time is ticking and you two are needed back on Earth. Lula, you must take them back to when you took them. We can't interfere in what is coming, but we can ensure their bond is strong."

A small burst of power filled Joni, healing her, linking her and Atlas. She hadn't realized she'd been thinking their lives wouldn't last past their time on Fey, but now as she met his blue eyes, she'd imagined him leaving her. "I never would've left you, Achwahnaja," Atlas rumbled, his bear making the claim as well.

"What about your clan, will they accept me if I'm not like you?" she asked, her deepest fear laid out before them all.

Atlas touched his nose to hers. "You're the only one most like me. I'm a dire; you're a dire. If they don't accept you, then we'll create our own clan, taking in all those who are different, kind of like Hollis and Annie. There are bound to be others who don't fit into the mold of clans. We will find them and offer them a place to belong."

"And that, is why you will be the true alpha the White Bear Clan needs," both Goddesses said simultaneously.

"I'll take them back now. Should I take them back to Texas, Mystic, or to White Bear?" Lula asked.

"Trouble is headed to Wolfs Run. We can't intercede there, so that's where they're needed."

Joni watched as her Goddesses eyes went milky white. "Yes, I agree. We will see you soon. Jenna is on her way."

"Ah, we must go, she's got her little ones and mates with her. No need to scare them. Silly men, they fear feminine power."

Again, the air shimmered, but Joni was sure she saw both Goddesses wink before they left the meadow.

"Did that really just happen?" she asked, swinging her head back toward the two towering dragons.

Lula leaned against her mother, both dragons looking drained.

"Yes, yes it did. Looks like your mating was destined and my child isn't in trouble, yet. Oh, goodie, look who's joined the party." Belle tilted her head to the side.

Joni thought the way both dragons moved was very smooth, almost reptilian like, but she'd keep that to herself.

"Too late, remember I can read your mind." Belle tapped her head, making Joni groan.

"Well, lookie here, it's a party and nobody invited me, the queen of this here darn realm," Jenna snarled. She stomped through the grass, her hand petting Joni as she passed. "Hello, gorgeous, I'll be right back.

"Jennaveve, be careful." A man snarled.

Joni blinked her eyes at the appearance of two men popping into the area, one with a baby strapped to his front with what appeared to be a baby carrier of some sort, only this one was purple and glittered when the sun hit it. The other had a matching one, only his baby was facing him instead of outward, clearly sleeping.

"If anyone comments about our choice in baby carrier, I'll suck you dry," he warned.

"Damien, be nice. They're purple and sparkly, therefore they're the best. Besides, who would ever say a negative word about them?" Jenna asked, her hands on her hips as she stopped in front of Belle.

Belle shifted to human, standing a little taller than Jenna. "I agree, they're quite lovely. However, pink would've been my choice."

Lula raised her hand, then put it down when Jenna pointed her finger at her. "Do not agree with your mother. Now, what the flying monkey butts is going on here?"

The other male holding a sleeping baby laughed. "Sorry, I just love the way you've cleaned up your language since the prettiest little girls in the world was born. Isn't that right, love bug," he cooed toward the little girl in the carrier his brother wore, whose legs were kicking at his words.

Jenna sighed, turning back toward Belle and Lula. "Wanna fill me in on the goings on?"

Joni shifted back to human, happy when the jeans and T-shirt appeared on her without fail. "It's my fault actually, my queen."

When the tiny fey's head turned almost completely around, without her body following, making Joni have visions of the exorcist, she almost regretted her announcement.

"For fookssake, Jennaveve, stop that. We told you that is freaking us out. How do you think that's affecting those who don't love you like Lucas and I do?"

Atlas snorted, then tried to cover it up with a cough.

"Lucas and you are both morons. I don't have eyes in the back of my head, so sometimes in extreme situations, I need to see what's behind me, hence this." She twirled her finger around her head.

"Nope, it's still freaky as fook." Damien shook his head.

"Listen, saying fook is just weird, instead of fuck. I think we just teach the prettiest little girls in the world to do as we say, not as we do is a better action. I mean, we have sex, like all the time. Are we going to stop that because they'll think they can? Or, stop drinking alcohol because Willow and Piper think they can too?" Jenna tapped her toe on the grass, her head still turned at the unnatural angle.

The one she'd called Lucas shook his head. "You started it."

Jenna turned around completely, her head finally on the right way. "How? How did I start it?"

Damien began rocking his hips back and forth, singing a song Joni had no clue what it was, but was sure he'd messed up somehow.

"You say darn instead of damn all the time." Lucas ran his palm over the head of the baby girl snuggled against his chest.

"You also say freak instead of fuck, all the freaking time," Damien agreed, stopping mid song."

The baby in his arms clapped and blew a raspberry.

"See, she likes it when we agree." Damien clapped in front of his daughter.

"Fine, I might have done that on occasion, but I never used the words, and I quote," she paused, raising her hands in the air to make quotation motions. "Fook, or fookssake. Those are just stupid words. Now, let's just forget them and move on, mkay?" She waved at the baby, blowing a kiss before turning back toward Joni. "Instead of you explaining, how 'bout I take a looksie? It won't hurt and is much more expedient."

Joni looked to Atlas, checking for his opinion. He moved closer to her, giving her his strength, but two male growls stopped him from getting too close.

"Easy, mates, he's just wanting to reassure his female he's got her back. Now, let's see what transpired, shall we?" Jenna murmured.

Calmness fell over her as she felt the presence of the Fey Queen enter her being. Her wolf sat back, watching, allowing the strange female to walk through her memories, uncaring she saw more than just the past few weeks. Finally, when Jenna left, Joni stumbled and would've fallen if Atlas hadn't been there to catch her.

"Oh my, I am...words escape me at the abuse. So much pain. If I could kill that bastard, I would. I can erase your memories, make them go away if you'd like?" Jenna wiped a tear from below her eyelid.

The offer was so very tempting. "Thank you, but no, I'll keep them. I don't know what tomorrow might bring, but I know what yesterday was. I'm not going to allow those hurts to keep me down any longer. I've learned staying angry does nothing but keep you down. Being mad does nothing but keep you from being happy. I'm going to learn to forgive, maybe one day I can forgive my parents. Today isn't that day, but if there's one thing that I do know, it's that I love Atlas with my whole heart. It's something the people who were supposed to love me didn't do. Looking at all of you, I can see that same love radiating from one another. I want to know that love, to enjoy it. I want to be loved and cared for in the same way and give it back, because they are the ones that truly matter."

Chapter Thirteen

Joni bit her lip after saying what she felt. Goddess, she couldn't face Atlas. She'd just professed her love in front of a crowd of people.

Hard arms lifted her, turning her to face him. "I swear, you break my heart and put it back together again. I love you, too, Joni. I know I said those were fairytale words, but if how I feel is what love is, then it's true."

She wrapped her arms around his head, feeling his strength hold her in more ways than just the arms locking her to him. "Goddess, I love you more than I've ever thought possible." Her next words were swallowed by his mouth.

"Alright I hate to break this up, but you need to head on home to Earth, folks," Jenna said.

It took effort to pull away from Atlas's kiss. When she did, both of their lips were puffy and wet, making her wish they were alone.

"Word of warning, if you were alone here, you'd end up with multiple pups, or cubs," Damien's deep voice warned.

Joni wiggled in Atlas's arms. "That would be a no from me," she laughed.

"Oh, I'll have to figure out a cute nickname for your offspring." Jenna tapped her nose, but a small wail from the baby in the carrier had her spinning toward the child. "Oh, what's the matter? Are you hungry?"

"Yep, it's feeding time, and sadly, you're the only one with the goodies." The man carrying the baby waggled his eyebrows. "Isn't she, my little lovenug?" His voice dropped to a comical one. The wailing child woke the other, making both babies cry.

Jenna turned to face Joni and Atlas. "I swear, that male comes up with a different nickname every darn...I mean damn hour." She smiled fondly. "Alright, let's get you two big bad dires back to Earth, so I can pop my boobs out and feed those two little miss thangs over there."

"Damn, when you say shit like that, it gets me hard," the other male said, adjusting himself.

Again, Jenna faced Joni, placing both hands around her mouth. "Like that's new," she mock whispered.

"I heard that," he said.

"Duh, I said it loud enough even the minotaur's heard it three counties over," she answered.

Both men looked around them, each moving so their backs faced one another. Both produced a shield that encapsulated the child strapped to his chest, leaving their arms free, which now wielded a sword that looked as if it could slice a solid rock in half. "Are these beasts' friend or foe?" Damien asked.

"Oh for the love of all that is fey, of course they're friends. Hello, you're in my realm." Jenna tossed her hands in the air.

The first little girl seemed to enjoy pressing on the bubble, her excited giggles could be heard through it. The other looked upward, her excited laughter at whatever was going on around her clearly not upsetting.

"Um, could you zap us home, or beam us back?" Atlas asked, his impatience clear.

"Goddess, you men are all alike. Now, do you require the happy juice my bestie Kellen does? You know, for the tummy 'cause you men are not made of sterner stuff like us females?" Jenna tilted her head slightly, acting as if she was saying the weather was a bit chilly, when in fact she just called into question the man's manhood.

It took everything Joni had not to burst into laughter as her mate puffed out his chest, knowing he was going to deny the need for any assistance. However, he let out a breath and nodded, taking Joni's hand in his.

"I'd appreciate any help you can offer. I need to be at one hundred percent when we get home. I don't want any handicaps in case I need to battle. My mate's life and happiness come before any male posturing," he intoned.

Joni wanted to launch herself at him, make both their clothes disappear, climb him like a spider monkey, and beg him to fuck her hard. Hell, she wouldn't even care if they created a damn baseball team if they all turned out like their father. Damn the amazing dire white bear.

"I fucking love you too, boo," he joked.

"I'm gonna have to ask you to no on the *boo*, boo bear," she said, shaking her head adamantly. The sexy man could call her many things, but boo, boothang, boobear; basically, anything that started with boo was a no for her.

Atlas pulled her in for a hug, kissing the tip of the nose. "Duly noted, Achwahnaja."

Lula gave a dramatic sigh. "I just love it when you males use words that are made up."

A deep laugh bubbled out of Atlas before he faced Lula. "Achwahnaja means love in my people's native language," he explained.

"Okay," Lula agreed, making the universal sign for okay while giving a dramatic wink. Clearly the dragon female didn't believe her mate, but that was alright with Joni.

"All aboard. The Fey Train is leaving. I'm gonna need you to close your eyes, count to three, and think of something nice, but not sexy nice. I do not need to see you and your mate getting it on." Jenna had her right arm bent and lifted, then at ear splitting level, she yelled, "toot toot." She laughed. "I've always wanted to do that."

"Yeah, well that will be the first and last time anyone says riding the Jenna, or Fey Train, woman. Do you have any idea what that means on Earth?" Lucas growled.

The Fey Queen squinted at both men. "Is this another thing humans have turned dirty?"

"I'm afraid so, mia cara," Damian said.

Joni squinted at Jenna. "Why do you need us to do that? Lula just sort of popped us here."

Jenna shrugged her shoulders. "I just like yelling all aboard and shit. Come on." She snapped her fingers.

They hurried over to Jenna, both unsure if she was kidding or not. Joni grabbed ahold of Atlas as the ground began to move, feeling as if she was being sucked into a vortex. "This feels way different then when Lula did it, too."

"That's cause I like to do it with a bit more pomp and flash. Ps. You're welcome. Byeeee," Jenna laugh, the sound, almost musical, made Joni want to close her eyes and listen to her forever. Goddess, the female was strange, yet wonderful.

The next moment, she felt solid ground beneath them. "Oh, we're home. It looks like time hasn't changed, or else it's the same time days later. Shoot, which do you think it is?"

Atlas glanced around the cornfield, trying to get his bearings. He didn't feel like retching, which he counted as a blessing. "One way to find out." He nodded toward the big farmhouse where Hollis and Annie lived.

Joni gave his fingers a slight squeeze. "Let's do this."

Oh yeah, she was his mate. Perfect in every way for him. He took off at a pace that she could keep up with, his long legs eating up the ground. He inhaled, checking for scents that didn't belong. With his mate next to him, he wouldn't take chances like he'd done in the past. Before, he hadn't bothered worrying about enemies lurking behind every tree or building. In his mind, if he'd been taken out, it would've been the Goddesses plan. Now however, he'd take out anyone who tried to harm one hair on Joni's precious head. Cavemanish maybe, but she was more important than his entire clan.

"I can feel the hairs on my arms tingling, Atlas. Something is coming and coming soon," she said.

He had the same feeling. Of course, the Goddess had said the same thing, but he hoped they had at least enough time to prepare for whatever it was that was going to come down. "Do you have a connection with Hollis or Annie? Can you reach out to them without alerting anyone else?" Being connected to the alpha would help them assess the situation, whereas if he reached out to him his presence might be felt since he was an outsider.

"I never became a full member of their crew. They would've let me, but something held me back," she whispered.

"If we shift, I can block our power from being broadcasted to other shifters." He looked up at the fading sun. Unlike the fairytales, shifters weren't held to the call of the moon. However, wolves felt a bigger pull to it than others. He wondered how Joni's beast would react since tonight was the first full moon.

"Do you think its safe for everyone if we shift into our dires? I don't want to go on an eating rampage." Joni's true fear shone in her shiny green gaze as she stared up at him.

He pushed her long black hair back from her face. "No, I don't believe you'll be in a frenzy to eat any and all things on two or four feet. Like you in either of your forms before, I believe your wolf might be a vegan," he joked.

Joni punched his arm, then sobered. "Let's do this, bossy bear."

He nodded. "Who's the bossy bear now?" He sobered as the need to get to the farm became urgent. "Follow me and please, for the love of all, stay next to me. If I have to look for you, my bear will be distracted, which could get someone hurt or killed." What he meant was he would put her and her safety first and foremost.

She nodded, then shifted before him. Atlas waited until her transformation was complete, running his hands through her thick fur. "Goddess, you're gorgeous. My turn." He then shifted, rubbing up against her on all sides, making sure she carried his scent as well as his mark on her shoulder. Any fool would see who her mate was, but he wanted to make sure they could smell the same thing.

They took off at a fast pace, their huge beasts eating up the distance. Atlas kept his senses open, his link to Joni showed she too was searching for enemies. The only smells were the Wilde Crew and livestock. However, he did smell fresh kills, like a slaughter had happened recently. *Do the Wilde's eat what they raise here?* he asked through their mating link.

"I don't know. It never came up, but it would make sense."

He veered around the perimeter of the property, checking where he scented the fresh kills, not finding any animals. After another circuit, they went to the back door. He shifted first, waiting for Joni to do the same. *"They're awake and alone, I'll knock, but stay behind me."*

After shifting, she stood on her tiptoes and gave him a kiss on his cheek. "Yes, sir, bossy bear."

His growl echoed around the quiet afternoon. He lifted his fist and rapped on the door twice. "Yo, Hollis."

The door opened; a weary looking Hollis stood in the entry. "Come on in, we were wondering how long you'd run around the property."

Atlas raised a brow. "What's going on?"

Annie leaned against the counter. "Well, you've been gone for less than an hour, but somehow, we've lost a dozen cattle." Accusation laced her tone.

Joni shook her head. "That's not right, Annie, and you know it. We've been gone a lot longer than that. Where's Lula?" She looked around the room.

"The crazy pink haired girl? She left shortly after you did, but not before threatening us. Who the hell was she, or rather what was she?" Annie snarled, fur popping up on her arms.

"I need you both to calm down and listen to me. This is going to sound crazy, but Joni and I have been gone for more than a day. Once Joni shifted into her new form, Lula took the both of us to the Fey Realm out of fear she'd be unstable. We returned here because—well trouble is coming, or rather has already arrived here. We need to prepare for battle," Atlas warned.

"It looks like trouble has already come, and it's standing in my kitchen, boy," Hollis growled. "What kind of bullshit you trying to sell me?"

Atlas growled back, pushing Joni behind him. "You're an alpha. You should be able to sense any lies. What did you smell when I was speaking?"

Hollis shook his head. "Fuck." He spun around, staring out at the field behind his home. "Then who killed my livestock?"

"I don't know, but I intend to find out. Have you called your crew in?" Atlas asked.

"Of course, I did. They're on the look out for you and Joni. I'm surprised they didn't kill the both of you on sight."

Chapter Fourteen

Joni gasped. "Why would they do that?"

Annie snarled. "Because they think you brought him here to kill us all and take over."

"For what gain, what purpose? That doesn't even make sense," Joni yelled back.

"Maybe you're working with Mikey. The asshole always wanted what I've had, especially my land and my mate." Hollis turned back around; his eyes bluer than before as his coyote was closer to the surface.

"That bastard was a creep. You know I have nothing to do with him, Annie." Joni held her hand out toward the other female. When she didn't acknowledge her words, she let her arm drop. "I can't believe you're both going to dismiss all the time I was here with you, all the...feelings I had for all of you. I thought you said I was like family, a part of your crew?" She dashed her hands beneath her eyes, hating the show of weakness.

"Oops, am I late? Did someone die?" Lula asked.

Annie tripped over the chair, falling on her ass. "Oh, my bad. Here, let me help you up." Lula grabbed Annie under both arms, easily hefting her into the air, settling her onto her feet. "So, what did I miss? Like I said, sorry I'm late. I had mama drama. Not baby mama drama 'cause I ain't got no baby, but ya know, my mama and drama. Lord love a duckling, that woman can rage and rage. Sheesh, you shoulda seen the smoke coming out of her nose. I swear she would've burned a village down if she didn't love the people of Fey so much. Anyhoo, I'm babbling." Lula rubbed her hands together, looking around the room at everyone.

"Hello, Lula. I'm glad you didn't get into too much trouble. Could you please inform these two exactly where we've been for the past twenty-four hours, give or take?" Atlas asked, folding his arms over his massive chest.

Joni moved closer to her mate, feeling lost once again. "Hi, Lula, thanks for showing up. I think we might need the backup in more ways than one. Both Atlas and I sense something big coming, and no, we're not saying you and your dragon are big, however she is magnificent," she assured the female. After knowing the slight framed female for such a short time, she'd learned Lula loved compliments.

"Look at you, you're a fast learner. Twenty points in your notebook." Lula pretended to write in an invisible book, or so Joni assumed it was pretend. It was hard to tell with the dragon.

"Alright, here we go, coyote and his less than stellar mate. Close your eyes and prepare yourselves for the greatest show on Earth, starring my friend and almost friend, Joni and Atlas," she yelled.

Joni snorted, unable to help herself when Lula moved forward, grabbing hold of Hollis and Annie, her hands holding their heads together. Although she could see Hollis tried to fight Lula's hold, he couldn't win against a dragon and her strength. Both Wilde's eyes widened, shock lining their features.

Lula stepped back. "I shouldn't have had to show you that. You should've trusted, which goes to show you that you are not their real people. However, these two are going to protect you and yours 'cause they're awesome like that. Now, the battle is upon us. Lets go people, move it, move it." Lula clapped her hands, lifting her legs comically high in the air as she marched toward the back door, looking over her shoulder she waved. "You coming or what?"

"Fuck, let's do this." Atlas cracked his neck. "Do I have your word you got my back, or do I need to worry you and your crew are going to fuck me and my mate over?" he asked.

Hollis shook his head. "I'm sorry for doubting you or Joni." He held his hand out. "You have my word we will fight alongside you, to the death if need be. Annie, go to the safe room. I need to know you're alright."

Annie licked her lips. "No, this is my fight, too. She's like the daughter we never had, yet we turned our back on her at the first chance. I will not do it again. Joni, I'm...I'm not worthy to call you daughter, but please know I do love you. I'll fight just as you."

"I don't want to see any of you die, but I do thank you for fighting with us. I'm not sure what's coming, but it feels big," she warned.

"We're ready," Thadd said through the screen.

"Let's move this out to the training area. It'll give us more room and less shit to fix," Hollis suggested.

"Good idea," she agreed. "My dragon will totally decimate this lovely home." Lula stepped past the gaping couple, shoved past the lion, and began walking toward the area they pointed at. "You coming or what? The Wicked are coming, and they're coming fast."

Atlas lifted his head, his nose flaring. "Son-of-a-bitch," he swore.

"What is it?" Joni took a deep breath. "Is that bear I smell?"

Oakland inhaled. A deep growl rumbled from him. "It sure the fuck is, and they're angry as hell. What did you bring here, girl?"

Atlas stepped in front of Oakland. His large frame a couple inches taller than Oakland's. "She brought nothing. This is all on me. My old alpha's mate clearly doesn't like the fact I found my truemate, and that she's a wolf. I plan to teach her, and whoever she talked into coming with her, a lesson. You with me?"

Joni held her breath as Oakland stared at Atlas. The entire Wilde Crew, made up of over fifteen shifters including Hollis and Annie, all nodded. "Absofuckinglutely," Oakland said, taking a step back shaking his arms out.

"Everyone shift. That way we know who is who when the shit hits the fan," Hollis suggested.

Atlas gave a humorless laugh. "Trust me, you'll know who is from the White Bear Clan when they arrive."

Hollis tilted his head in question.

"They'll all be grizzly bears for one, for another, they'll each smell as if their shit doesn't stink, but they do," Atlas laughed.

"Shift, crew," Hollis ordered.

The entire Wilde Crew shifted, their bones cracking, skin stretching not nearly as seamless as when Joni and Atlas did, yet when they finished, each shook out their coats, stood on four legs and held their heads high.

"Alright, I'm going to link all of you with a linkyloos so you can all talk to one another. Okie dokie?" Lula asked. I won't shift unless I need to. I'm kinda a badass in this form, so don't worry your furry little heads about me." She patted Joni's flank.

If one could roll their eyes in wolf form, Joni was sure she just did. The sound of thunder broke through the night. She looked to the sky, finding it to be clear and full of stars. *"Looks like the party is getting ready to start. We taking the front or the back?"* Joni asked.

She noticed the Wilde Crew had gone quiet.

"Is there a problem?" Atlas asked through the link Lula had created.

"Holy sheot, girl. What the hell happened to you? Did you eat all your damn vitamins or what? Like, fucking hell, you can wipe the floor with all of us and still say 'Next,'" Thadd said, awe in every word.

Joni's wolf stood a little taller. *"I am pretty big, yeah?"*

Two wolves she'd met during training flanked her. *"Big doesn't even come close to describing you. And white. You're the thing of myths."*

Joni stared down at Erica and Kyle, the mated pair, giving them a slight bow. *"Thank you, but I'm just a regular wolf who happens to be mated to a dire bear."*

"Like we said, a wolf of myths. A dire wolf is legendary. We will fight alongside you with pride, Joni." Kyle tilted his head to the side, showing his submission, his mate following his lead.

Joni opened her wolven mouth to lick them both, but just then, the world around them exploded as a couple dozen bears surrounded them.

She spun to find Atlas charging a huge bear, taking him down with a swipe of his paw. Sexy, bossy bear.

The ground shook as the bears raced toward her and her friends. Joni faced her enemies, vowing she would kill each and every bear who dared to harm them. She opened her mouth, howling loudly. Instead of letting them come to her, she allowed her wolf to take over, feeling her rake at her mind with the need to protect.

The first bear she faced, Joni was elated to see she was larger than, taking it down easily, her teeth locking on its exposed throat while Erica and Kyle locked onto its legs. The three of them worked as a pack, killing it and then moving to the next. They moved swiftly and efficiently, maiming and killing bear after bear. She heard a pained howl, then looked back to see Erica lying on her side with a smaller bear standing over her. It's huge paw ready to come down on her friend with a killing strike.

A blur of black ran in front of Joni, latching onto the bear's arm, only to be shook off like a nuisance. Joni used the distraction, rushing the bear, knocking them both onto their sides. She looked back, meeting Erica's hazel eyes, her pain filled Joni with purpose. She hustled to gain her feet, facing off against the grizzly. Hate stared back at her through the female's eyes.

All around them, grunts and the smell of blood filled the air, but her sole focus was the grizzly in front of her. Atlas had said they'd know who the enemy was by their scent. Joni had no doubt the female in front of her was the old alpha's mate. She was larger than the other bears Joni had faced, but that wasn't what set her apart. This bear wore a medallion around her neck. Joni tilted her head to the side, wondering how she'd kept it on during her shift. However, before she could work it out, she was slammed into from the side. The hit felt as though a diesel had plowed into her. Before she could gain her feet, the first bear gripped her by the scruff of her neck, carrying her like a cub and took off at a clip Joni didn't think a bear of her size could do.

"Atlas," she cried out through their link before a sharp pain cut into her mind and then darkness surrounded her.

Atlas took out another traitor from his clan, his bear easily decimating the stupid males. He looked around the clearing, shocked at the amount of damage they'd wrought. When there was only one grizzly still standing, looking a little worse for wear, but clearly on their side, he sighed. *"Is everyone alright?"* he asked through the link.

His bear wanted to rip every last one of them to shreds, but as the alpha he also knew he needed to give the clan closure. The sound of his mate calling out to him through their mating link had him freezing, his entire focus turning toward the road. *"Did anyone see where Joni went?"*

Erica and Kyle lay on the ground closest to the edge of the clearing, the female bleeding profusely was worrisome, but his focus was on his mate. He shifted, hurrying to where they were. "What happened?"

Kyle shifted, facing Atlas. "I'm sorry, Alpha, Erica was injured. I was batted off like a fly, and then Joni attacked, but she was blindsided by another bear from the side. They took off faster than I thought a bear could move," Kyle swore.

Atlas knew who had his mate. The only female who would dare try to take what was his, the bitch who wanted to be alpha. Matilda, the crazy female thought she should be the one to run the clan. "I can find her." Even though their link was being blocked, his dire bear was connected to Joni on a level even crazy Matty couldn't severe. Nothing could, except death, and that was something Atlas wouldn't allow to happen.

He searched for Lula, finding the dragon female lifting several bears into her arms at once with the Wilde Crew looking on with their mouths gaping open. "Lula, I need you," he bellowed.

Lula paused with her arms full. "One sec." She disappeared, taking the entire bear clan with her. Seconds later, she reappeared, her face grim. "The White Bear Clan thanks all of you for your service and await their true alpha's return with his truemate by his side."

It was the first time he'd heard Lula speak so formally and wondered how long she'd actually been gone, knowing she had a way of manipulating time. "Thank you, Lula, I owe you a debt, many debts," he vowed.

She shook her head. "No, you owe me nothing but to be a good mate to Joni. Now, let's go get our girl away from the nasty beotches." She rubbed her hands down her legs. "Getting rid of bodies is such a dirty job, but someone has to do it. Many of the ones who were here only came because she was their alpha's mate. I would've saved them had they stopped when I reached out to them, but they feared her worse than they feared me." She shrugged.

"Lula," he said her name with impatience. If Matilda had too much time, she'd kill Joni without remorse.

"Alright, let's go, bossy bear." Lula stomped past him, grabbing his arm.

Atlas growled. "Only Joni has the right to call me that."

"Fine, big ass bear, follow me," Lula agreed.

He could smell gas and burned rubber from where the vehicle had clearly taken off in a hurry. "Shit, we're too late." He hung his head.

"Aw, don't fret, my little bear." Lula patted his arm. "I know which way to go."

His world went dark before she finished speaking, making him wonder if he should ask for something to vomit in. Less than a minute later, he blinked to find himself inside a damp cave that smelled oddly familiar. "What the hell?" he muttered.

"Sssh, they'll be here momentarily. They've actually been here for a few days staking out the place just lying in wait for you and Joni to show up, devious bear females."

He couldn't deny her words. The sickening smells had his beast raking at his insides, while the man in him wanted to deny what they knew. At the sound of a vehicle, he and Lula moved further into the cave, which was such a cliché he wanted to roar his anger.

"I've masked both of our scents so they wouldn't know we're here. However, I can't interfere in what is to come, only you and your mate can be a party to the events that unfold." Lula folded her arms in front of her, her words inside his head a reminder they were still linked.

"I will forever be in your debt for what you've done for me and my mate, Lula. If you ever have need of me or my clan, you only have to reach out to me, and I'll do what I can to help," he said, placing his fist over his chest.

Before Lula could answer, the cave's entrance was filled with Matilda, followed by Sonya who was dragging an unconscious Joni by her hair. Atlas took a step, but Lula pressed her palm into his chest. *"Wait, there is another."*

It grated to watch his mate be treated in such a way, but he did as Lula suggested. Another minute passed, and then a huge man entered the cave, one he recognized as the father of the child bride they'd wanted him to mate with. "So, that's the bitch your son chose over my daughter?"

"As you can see, we've contained the problem." Matilda walked toward the alpha of the Red River Clan.

"How does this contain it? Where is your son, the alpha? How is he to mate with my daughter if he is not here and willing?" Adon Kline growled.

Sonya stepped over Joni, seeming to not care about her in the least as she ran a hand down Adon's chest. "Well, you see, we plan to lure my son here so you can kill him. We'll kill his mate, and then you can mate with us, creating a triad the likes of which our clan has never seen."

Atlas had to shake his head at his mother's words. They thought Adon could kill him, then the three of them take over the clan? Not only were they delusional, they clearly had been planning something like this for a while.

Adon laughed. "Why would I mate with the two of you?"

Matilda stepped forward. "You'd get two mates who would see to your every need. Don't you have needs, Adon? Have you ever wanted to watch two women pleasure each other while you watched? We can give you that and more. More ecstasy than you can ever imagine," she purred.

Before the females could make good on what they were saying, he stepped forward. If he had to watch the woman who gave birth to him make out with another female, or male, he didn't think he'd be able to stomach it.

"I get to rip the throat out of that bitch Matilda," Joni whispered through their link.

He wanted to smile at the angry snarl in his mate's tone. *"Agreed. You need to follow my lead, Achwahnaja."*

"They plan on killing him after he agrees to mate them. Not today or anytime soon, but once your clan accepts him. Oh, they will mourn, of course," she sneered.

He wanted to question her more about what she'd learned, but the trio were getting a little too handsy with each other. With deliberate loudness, he stepped into the opening. "Well, isn't this—disturbing?"

Chapter Fifteen

If he could take a picture for all time, he'd have taken one of the shocked expressions on the two females' faces at his appearance. "Hello, mother, you're looking, scandalous."

His words were clearly not appreciated as she tried to cover her assets, which she'd put out for Adon's benefit. "What the hell are you doing here, Atlas?" she asked.

"What the hell is going on?" Adon boomed.

Atlas tossed his head back, laughing at the entire situation. "Let's see. The three of you are planning my demise, while also preparing to kill my mate. Afterward, you'll take over as the alpha and his mates, combining both clans, making it the largest bear clan in North America. Am I close?" He allowed his bear to push forward, knowing if he had to shift he'd have to do it faster than he'd ever done before. Luckily for him, the cave was large enough for his dire bear, and Joni to shift easily and still be able to fight the three other shifters unhindered.

"You can't kill us, Atlas," Matilda warned.

He shifted closer to where Joni lay, her breathing steady as if she was still knocked out. "And why is that?" he questioned, stalling for time.

Matilda pulled a chain from around her neck. "This gives me power over you and her. I can control your shifts, and your bear and her wolf. You see, even though you're the great white bear, you can be brought to your knees by a bauble. Go ahead, try shifting," she dared him.

He wasn't going to give her the satisfaction of shifting. If she wanted him to shift, there was a reason, which meant he would do the opposite, unless that was what she wanted him to do. Fuck, he hated riddles. Looking at the female who'd birthed him gave nothing away, her hatred toward him was the same as always. "So, mom, you like to play for the other team, huh? How'd dear old dad take that news, or was he into that kinkery too? Not that I'm judging or anything. Love is love in my mind, but you and she don't appear to love one another."

"You were always a little bastard, even when you were only hours old. I hated you on sight. Most babies come out crying, but you came out quiet, looking at me like you knew what I was thinking, your eyes accusing me of past deeds. Then you'd take your punishments, and you'd look at me as if it was my fault. My fault," she screeched, launching herself at him.

Joni popped up off the ground, her hand wrapping around Sonya's throat. "You are the worst excuse for a mother I've ever heard of. I've seen inside your mind and your heart. Oh, I saw what you did, what you allowed to happen to him as a child. For that alone, I, mate to Atlas, future mother to his wolf-bear cubs, sentence you to death." Joni didn't allow her a chance to speak, or fight. Her dire wolf rose quickly and deadly, partially shifting, ripping Sonya's head from her body with her other hand.

"What have you done?" Matilda screeched.

Joni dropped what was left of Atlas's biological mother. "Made the Earth a better place. Ready to go next, bitch?"

Atlas seriously thought his mate was sexy as fuck in her partial shift. His own dire bear wanted to wrap his arms around their female, but he caught movement out of the corner of his eye. Adon was on the move. He knew if the male left, he'd return with his clan, maybe not today, or even in a week, but he'd always have to watch his back. With a roar that shook the cave walls, he shifted, taking the alpha down, the fight took less than thirty seconds. When he turned back, he found Joni standing over Matilda who held the strange necklace in her hands, a smirk on her face.

"I can still stop you both," she said.

Joni looked to him; her form shimmered back to human. "I'm in full control of my body, how about you?"

Atlas tried to shift back to his human self, but found he wasn't able. *"No, I'm stuck like this."*

"Unless he wants to be a dire bear for the rest of his miserable life, I suggest you both let me go. Once I'm free of you, I'll release him from my hold." Matilda glared up at Joni.

Joni pinned the other woman down with her body straddling her, but she didn't dare take the necklace from her. "How does that work? We're just supposed to believe if we let you go, you'll lift the curse or whatever? Or is it proximity?"

"My blood releases the binding," she gasped, looking around the space.

Lula stepped out. "I couldn't fight the battle, but I can make her tell the truth. Now, prick her finger and take the necklace." Lula pointed at Matilda.

Joni grabbed the chain and yanked, uncaring of the pain it caused the female. She shifted one hand, claws bursting from the tips of her fingers. "This is so cool," she exclaimed, amazed at the ease she was finding in her new form. While Matilda struggled beneath her, she used her pointer finger to slice open Matilda's cheek, the blood welling up enough to soak the medallion. "Now what?" she looked at Lula.

"Or slicing her cheek works too, I like how you work. Now you say something like, you release the dire bear, or whatever." Lula shrugged.

Joni wanted to strangle the tiny female, but the fact she was a dragon kept her in place. "You're released from whatever bindings that held you, forever," she tacked on.

Atlas groaned, then he shifted, becoming the sexy man Joni loved. "Holy shit, I don't ever want to be stuck in one or the other ever again."

He shut his mouth with an audible snap. "Damn, forget I said that, love."

She shook her head, then thinking the necklace in her hands could be dangerous, she crushed it in her palm. "Lula, can you like melt this down to nothing?"

Lula held her hand out. "It would be an honor. I'll also gladly melt that nasty one, if you'd like." She tilted her head toward Matilda who'd begun to shift below Joni.

Joni jumped backward as the female became a grizzly, huge paws swiping out trying to take off anything in her vicinity.

Atlas pushed Joni behind him, his body shifting, claws larger than the female's head sliced through her neck. In one swipe, he ended Matilda and her reign of terror. He turned his back, not watching as the body fell lifeless onto the dirt floor of the cave.

Joni could see how much he hated what they'd had to do today, but deep within her mate's heart and mind, they both knew if they hadn't faced the battle in Texas, they'd have done so on their clan's land. "It's done. We can go home now, Atlas."

"Where is our home, Joni? Where do you want to go?" he asked.

She walked up, wrapping her arms around the huge bear of a man who'd stolen her heart all those months ago. "My home is where you are, bossy bear. I read once that we should all count our blessings by the things we have. Well, here's what I plan to do once we get to White Bear Clan. First, I think we need to rethink that name, since you know, I'm not a bear and not every bear there is white. It seems wrong to call it that, don't you think? Anyhoo, back to my words of wisdom. There are those who only think to measure their wealth when they have money or things they count as worthy. However, I want to count other things. For instance, counting my garden which I plan to have by the amount of flowers I can grow. Each day that I can make you smile, or another person smile instead of cry, I plan to count that, too. Each new season I get to spend with you, I want to celebrate and count that as a blessing, instead of another season that has passed. You see, all these things are blessings I want to cherish with you, bossy bear."

A sniff had Joni looking past Atlas. "That was one of the loveliest things I've ever heard. How about I give you a lift to the clan that has yet to get renamed?" Lula exclaimed.

"Shit, that's gonna take some thinking," Atlas said.

Joni patted his hand. "We'll figure it out. Besides, you've got family to help right?"

He groaned. "Fuck, how do I tell them about this?" He waved toward the body of Sonya and Matilda.

Lula raised her hand. "Let me handle it, mkay?"

****

Joni was a little worried about letting Lula handle the explaining to Atlas's brothers and sister, but as soon as she popped them into the middle of the alpha house where the three siblings were sitting, her fears dissipated. Not only were Abyle and Atika okay with their mother's death, they had eyes, and clearly hearts, for the pink haired dragon.

"You're sure she's not going to rise from the dead?" Shauny asked, her back to them all.

"Nope, she's deader than a...doornail." Lula held up her hand. "Why do humans say that? I mean, are doornails alive? Were they ever alive? It makes absolutely no sense whatsoever. Anyhoo, must be going now," she muttered, edging backward.

"You're ours, female," Atika snarled.

Lula shook her head. "Nope, not yours, or yours, but my own."

Before either man could reach her, Lula disappeared, leaving the room deathly quiet.

"Well, fuck. That's not who I thought would be our mate," Abyle whispered.

Atika punched a hole in the wall. "What the hell do you mean?"

Abyle stared at the space Lula stood. "She's not a bear."

Shauny turned to face them. "What is she? I couldn't sense what exactly she was, but she seemed—off."

Joni looked at Atlas, waiting for him to explain. "Lula is not from Earth, boys. I think it's best you forget about her and look for your mate or mates elsewhere."

His brothers turned toward him. Each lifted their lips in a snarl. "Would you have left Joni alone and found another?"

Atlas pulled her in front of him. He'd done just that, leaving his heart in shreds and knew it was asking his brothers to do the same. However, his mate was not the same as a dragon from a realm that was inaccessible to them. Hell, the Goddess could've ended him for stepping one paw on her space even though Lula had taken him there. "Joni's different from Lula. She was attainable. I...I'm not sure how to explain to you what Lula is. Hell, I'm not sure I can tell you. First things first, we need to fix this clan. I'm going to need the strength of my family to do it."

Abyle and Atika took deep breaths, each of them looking as if they were preparing for battle. "We will help you settle the clan. Once our job is done, we are going to find our mate."

Joni knew she'd do all she could to help them, but first she had to support Atlas and her new clan. "We'll do all we can."

The twins nodded; their jaws set in determined lines. He pulled each of them in for a hug, not the kind you'd give a man that was an acquaintance, but a brother he loved. The hard embraces lasted seconds, but their bonds strengthened. "We'll get through this like family are supposed to do." He pulled back, meeting each man's intense stare. They had the dark eyes of their mother, but none of the hatred.

"We've always had your back, brother," Abyle agreed. His twin squeezed Atlas's shoulder one last time before they turned toward the door, leaving together like they'd always done.

"I'll see you two in the morning. I suggest you call a clan meeting after you have breakfast and introduce your mate. Sorta like ripping the band aid off right away. If there are going to be any that aren't happy with who the Goddess chose as your truemate—well, let them speak up." Her eyes brightened, showing him the alpha female, she hid beneath the thin veneer of pristine clothing. His little sister was going to be one hell of a handful for her mate.

Once his family had gone, Atlas took Joni to the suite that was now his and hers. In the time he'd been away, Shauny had cleaned out all the old alpha's things and replaced it with new, adding things of his to make him feel more at home. "My sister is amazing," he told Joni.

"She seems sad, though. Almost like she's lost the love of her life?" Joni ran her hands up his chest.

His body responded to her every caress. "I don't think so. If she'd found a mate, Sonya would've had her mated and with cub in no time flat," he muttered.

Joni gripped his face between her palms. "Not if he wasn't a match that would've benefitted the clan, or wasn't the perfect bear, or goddess forbid, not a bear at all."

Atlas sucked in a breath. His mate's words hitting him like a bolt. Fuck, if his sister had found a mate that the bitch who'd birthed them didn't find suitable, Sonya would've done anything she felt necessary to keep them apart. "Goddess, I hope Shauny never let on who he was if that's true."

"We'll do what we can to help her," Joni said.

If Sonya found out her only daughter's mate was anything but what she deemed appropriate, Atlas didn't think there was any help for the unknown male or his sister. "Tonight, let's forget about everyone and everything except you and me," he suggested, lifting her into his arms, need rising in him like a storm.

Joni's smile lit up her face, her sweet arousal unmistakable as it perfumed the air. He inhaled, memorizing every single thing about his mate. "I like that idea. How about we make it a rule. When we enter our bedroom, nothing else comes in here. None of the stress or politics of pack or clan, or whatever we call our crew, interferes in our mating. In here, it's just you and me."

He smiled at that. Yeah, he liked that, liked the way his female thought, liked the way she lit up just for him and wanted to put them first, at least in their bedroom. Oh, he planned to take her whenever, however he wanted.

At the side of the specially made king bed, he set her on the mattress, taking her wrists in his, pushing them over her head. "Hold them here while I undress you. I have a need to take care of my mate." With slow deliberation, he ripped the top and bra she wore down the middle, making her gasp. Joni had large breasts, tipped with nipples made for sucking. He'd yet to give them the proper attention. Holding her eyes with his, he bent, licking the tip of one, then biting down on the hardened peak before moving to the other. "You like that?"

She nodded. "My nipples have always been sensitive."

He repeated the action on the other one, making her gasp. "I want to fuck your tits, but not tonight. They're perfect, fitting in my hands like they were made just for me." He lifted each one as he spoke, squeezing the firm flesh that would look amazing coated with his come.

"Are you trying to make me come before you even get to the good parts?" she panted.

He looked down her body, fascinated to see her chest rising and falling as if she'd run a marathon, and all he'd done was rip her shirt and bra in half, leaving the edges dangling from her shoulders. "You can come whenever you like, just as long as it's with me." Atlas wanted to taste her, every inch of her. Her mouth opened, but he was done talking. They had the rest of their lives to talk. Releasing one of her breasts, he gripped her hair in his fist, tilted her head back, and covered her lips with his, taking her mouth in a claiming kiss.

Joni's eyes closed, pleasure obvious on her face. She writhed against him, her chest moving against his, making him wish there was nothing between them.

He shifted his hand from her breast, ripping his own shirt off, uncaring he'd just destroyed both of their tops. When his bare chest met her naked one, they both sighed into the kiss. Still not satisfied, he worked her pants down her hips, tossing them off to the side. He broke away from her lips, biting on her bottom lip one last time. Her flushed cheeks had him bending for another lick inside. He leaned back, panting like a man who'd ran a marathon. "Scoot up to the middle, Achwahnaja," he muttered.

"Bossy bear," she laughed, but then she flipped over onto her hands and knees, crawling to the center of the bed, glancing over her shoulder. "Is this what you meant?" Her smile lit up her face as she turned onto her back, her hand running down her chest, stopping just below her belly button.

He ran his hands down his face. "Female, you're gonna be the death of me." Her sweet arousal soaked the tiny scrap of material between her thighs. He wanted to rip the silk material off with his teeth and keep it as a souvenir. "Did you know teal is my favorite color?" Atlas indicated with a jut of his chin toward the juncture between her thighs, seeing her hand run along the edge of the teal panties.

He worked his jeans down his legs, stepping out of them and then pushed his boxer briefs down, freeing his dick before he lost all feeling to the poor thing. Hell, watching his mate crawl across his bed nearly had him coming. His cock strained against the tight confines of the denim so much he feared he'd have imprints from the briefs along his shaft.

"Aw, poor baby. Does that hurt? Come here, I'll kiss him all better." Joni leaned up on her elbows.

Atlas mimicked her moves, crawling up on the bed, stalking his prey. "Ah, my little mate likes to play does she? Guess what, so do I, only I like to be the one in charge." He stopped with his face over her mound, inhaling deeply. "Your scent drives me wild."

"You drive me wild, Atlas. I'm yours to do with as you please," she whispered.

Fuck. His heart turned over with her simple words. Gratitude, love, hope, trust, and longing unlike any he'd known floored him. Gratitude that she wanted him as much as he wanted her. Love, the fact that she could have those feelings for a man whose own parents couldn't, amazed him. Hope for a future filled with him and her and any children they may have, no matter what species, and trust that she'd always have his back. Atlas never thought he'd find a mate, let alone one who was his truemate. He sent a silent prayer up to the Goddesses for gifting him his forbidden wolf, swearing he'd always love and protect her.

"Hey, where'd you go?" Joni's hand ran over his head.

He leaned into her touch, then kissed her stomach right above where her panties started. "One day, you'll carry our children. I swear, I'll love them unconditionally."

Joni felt her wolf go still. She wasn't sure if she was ready to become a mother. "Um, I know you will, but that won't be for a while, right?"

Atlas chuckled. "I'm not ready right this minute. Although, I do suggest we practice, you know...doing it. We want to get the technique down for when we do decide to make the most precious of children this world has ever seen."

She laughed at his words. "Most precious?"

Atlas kissed her again, his fingers working her panties down. She lifted her hips, helping him. "Of course, the most precious and most adorable. That is until they get older, then they'll become the most beautiful or handsome, depending on the sex. It's a shame really."

Joni was having a hard time following what he was saying as his tongue began licking a slow path between her spread thighs. "Holy shit, that feels amazing." Her ass lifted off the bed, wanting more, but he pressed her back down with one big palm on her stomach. "Why's it a shame?" she panted.

Atlas looked up from between her thighs, his fingers spreading her lower lips apart. She watched him blow warm air on her exposed flesh, shivering at the sensation. "Atlas, don't stop," she moaned.

"You asked me a question. It would be rude to not answer," he breathed against her. With another lick from her clit all the way to her ass, he seemed content to torture her. "It's a shame, because our children, the ones way in the future, are going to be the most gorgeous, the smartest, and clearly the strongest, fastest, the best at everything that it'll be hard for all other children to live up to such perfection." He grinned up at her, each sentence was ended with a lick or suck, sending Joni flying into an orgasm that had her screaming his name.

Panting, she pushed back the hair from her eyes. "You do realize you can't say that to anyone else, or they'll think you're an egotistical crazy man, right?"

Atlas gave her one last long lick, his face shining with her juices. "Don't care."

A laugh burst from her at his words. "Goddess, I love you."

"That's good to hear, love, since you're stuck with me for the rest of our lives and beyond. Now, I have a need to see you on your hands and knees again."

Her heart raced at the thought of him taking her from behind. Before she could get up, he flipped her over, slapping her on the right ass cheek. "Ouch," she yelped.

Atlas placed a kiss on the stinging flesh. "Your flesh looks good with my handprint on it."

His words had her squirming. "Is it bad that just made me hot?"

He knelt behind her, his left hand reaching around and between her thighs. "Achwahnaja, nothing, and I mean nothing we do together is wrong if we find pleasure in it. If ever I do or say something you don't like, you tell me, and we'll talk about it. I'll never do anything that hurts you. My entire life, I've only ever wanted to love and be loved. Now that I have you, I plan to spend the rest of my life being the best mate and one day father. Being the alpha is secondary to all of that. I'd walk away from the clan if your happiness was in question."

Joni pushed back against him, his words making her love him and want him all the more. "Make love to me, Atlas. I want you hard and fast this time. Next time, we can go slow and easy, but this time I need you. The raw you."

Her words seemed to set off his inner caveman. After checking she was wet, he slammed inside her, one hand holding her hip, his fingers digging into her flesh, leaving his marks there, the other was wrapped around her hair, holding her in place with her head turned to the side as if he needed to see her face. "Fucking love you, Joni."

"Ah shit, Atlas," she wheezed. Joni didn't try to break his hold. He was the alpha in their relationship. He needed to be in control, and she needed to give him this. His thrusts increased, sliding in and out, making her moan as his dick hit every tingly part of her that needed him. Shit, there wasn't a single thing he did she didn't love, even when he slowed, only to speed back up.

"I'm close, Konese," he growled. He released her hair, his hand moved between them, flicking her clit with his thumb.

Joni tensed beneath him, pushing backward. The firm tap had her tensing. "More," she said.

He chuckled. "Yes, ma'am," he answered.

She thought she was prepared, but when he pulled back, almost leaving her body, then slammed back inside, then repeated the action, again and again, his thumb flicking her clit at the same time, she could do nothing but come, his name spilling from her lips as lights danced behind her eyes. "Yes, Atlas," she screamed, back bowed, hips moving to meet his. "Fuck me."

"Loving you, always loving you," he rasped.

The warm feel of his come filling her sent another jolt of ecstasy through her already over sensitized body. He surged up, his teeth sinking into his mark, staking his claim all over again. She smiled, loving the feel of him covering her. If they went to sleep every night just like that, she'd be a happy female.

Her eyes closed, a smile on her face as he slipped from her body.

"Sleep, love, I'll take care of you." Joni thought she might've agreed, but tiredness had her drifting off to sleep.

Tomorrow, they were going to face his clan as the mated alpha pair.

Chapter Sixteen

Atlas looked down at his mate, his chest blooming with pride. The evidence of their joining trickled from between her thighs. He was tempted to leave it, but decided she'd sleep more comfortably if he cleaned her up. "I will start as I mean to go on," he whispered, a grin on his face.

For the first time in what felt like his entire life, he was happy. Tomorrow he'd face his clan with Joni by his side. If they didn't want to accept her as his mate, he'd step down and they could find another alpha. Hell, either one of his brothers would be excellent choices. He shrugged, waiting for the suffocating feel of doom to hit. He'd been brought up with the knowledge that his life was set to become the alpha. Now, because of one tiny slip of a female, he would gladly give it up for her and a life as her mate.

In the master bath, he was happy to see his sister had changed out all of the shit Matilda and the old alpha had in there as well. "You'll make a fine mate someday, Shauny." He shook his head, hoping like hell she hadn't already lost the chance.

He grabbed one of the fluffy teal towels, smiling at his sister's knowledge of his favorite colors. Shit, he hoped Joni liked it. Tomorrow, he'd find out and give her free reign. That is if they were still part of the clan. He turned the faucet on, waited until the water warmed before wetting the washcloth. He snagged a dry towel on the way out, stopping in the doorway at the vision of Joni lying on her back, her arm over her eyes. A female only slept totally abandoned like his mate if they were secure, if they felt safe. His chest swelled, knowing he'd given her that. "I'll always keep you safe," he promised.

With the warm cloth in hand, he leaned over the bed. Trying not to wake her, he eased it between her thighs. Her thighs opened, she moaned but didn't protest. He quickly wiped his come from between her legs, then dried her off, when what he really wanted to do was slide back where he'd been and get her all dirty again. Her heavy sigh kept him from acting on his impulse.

Tossing both rags through the open door to the bathroom, Atlas climbed in next to his mate, pulled the blanket from the bottom of the bed, curving his body around Joni's. Tonight, was going to be the first of many if he had anything to say about it.

Atlas woke, feeling something squeezing his cock. He lifted one eyelid, peering down to see his mate lying between his legs. "Good morning, sleepy bear."

"Mornin'," he rumbled. He tried to clear his throat so he could speak clearer. "What're you doing?"

Joni tightened her hold. "Well, if you have to ask, then I must not be doing it right." Her eyes sparkled.

He was prepared to tell her she was doing it just fine when she lowered her head, taking the head into her warm wet mouth, making any thought leave him.

"Shit, Joni," he breathed, his head pressed back into the pillow beneath him. He did his best not to thrust his hips forward when all he wanted to do was grab her head and fuck her face.

"Come here, let me taste you, too." He used his strength to maneuver her over his face, her gorgeous pussy the perfect breakfast for a bear. "Yes, I do so love your honey."

"Hey, I was the one who was enjoying my treat," Joni pouted.

He put one big hand on her back, urging her forward. "By all means."

The feel of her slim hand gripping him had his hips lifting. The next ten minutes was a game of who could get who off first, but neither of them was the loser as Joni learned just how he liked his dick sucked. "Damn, if you don't want me to come down your throat, you better stop," he warned. Her hand moved faster; her lips firmed as she urged him on. Atlas sucked her clit into his mouth at the same time his come exploded from him, her shouting his name, seconds after his dick stopped twitching, was music to his ears.

She lay with her head on his thigh, his dick licked clean. "Did I say good morning?" she asked.

Atlas laughed. He gripped Joni by the waist and lifted her up, shuffling her around until she lay beside him. "Good morning, mate."

A sound interrupted what she'd been ready to say, the scent of his sister and brothers letting him know they'd already arrived. "Sounds like duty calls. Want to shower with me?" Atlas gave her a kiss on the corner of her mouth.

"If you two shower together, you'll take forever," Shauny yelled through the door.

"Shauny, I will hurt you if you don't get away from my bedroom," he promised.

The sound of his sister's laughter trailed away. Joni's cheeks bloomed a becoming pink. "Goodness, she's going to know what we've been doing."

He kissed her forehead. "That's a good thing, Achwahnaja. Come on, lets conserve water." Atlas picked her up, tossed her over his shoulder, and carried her into the bathroom. Her squeak of delight had him grinning from ear to ear. "You have the sexiest little ass I've ever seen," he said.

Joni slapped his ass. "Oh really, and just how many asses are you comparing mine to?"

Atlas turned his head slightly, letting the stubble on his chin scrape her tender flesh, then nipped it. "I can't even picture any other but yours."

"Well, if we're talking about sexy asses, then I do declare yours is the finest I've seen as well." She pinched him on the opposite cheek. "Damn, son, I bet I could bounce quarters off of here."

Atlas laughed at her words. "I don't think we'll be finding out, love." He turned the taps on in the huge walk-in shower. Once the water was warm, he led Joni inside. Each side had shower heads, so while Joni stood under one, he stood under the other, watching her wash off. With her head back, her eyes closed, he thought she looked exactly as she had when he made her come.

"You keep staring at me like that, and you'll wake the monster," Joni said without opening her eyes, her hands working shampoo into her hair.

He lifted both brows. "What monster?"

"The one between your legs that promises to split me in two if I'm a bad girl, or maybe that's if I'm a good girl." She laughed, opening her eyes. "Or maybe it's a lollipop or an ice cream cone just waiting to be sucked, but," she paused, tapping her lip. "That can't be right, I already did that."

Atlas crossed the short distance, lifting her up by the waist. "I'll show you monster. Wrap your legs around me. We're supposed to be conserving water here, brat." He pressed her against the tile wall with his hips, taking her gasp into his mouth. Joni ground down on him, seeking her own pleasure.

"Yes, fuck me back, show me you like how I fuck you," he whispered. Her hips jerked, swiveling against him.

"Damn, why does that make me horny?" she whimpered.

He shifted back slightly, watching the way his dick slid in and out of her, letting her see as well. "Because you like hearing what I'm going to do to you, with you. That's right, move with me, just like that. Fuck, I can feel your pussy squeezing my dick, Joni, grind down on me again." He gripped her tighter against him, his fingers digging into her ass. "Come on my cock. Let me see my beautiful, sexy, dire wolf mate, coming for me."

"Oh yes, I'm coming." Her eyes brightened; her teeth lengthened.

Atlas felt his bear rake to claim. He tilted his neck, needing to feel her staking her claim on him again. Sharp canines entered his muscle, making him come. He lifted her up and down, feeling her orgasm rush over her at the same time. When her rough tongue sealed the wound on his shoulder, he tugged her head to the side, sliding his own teeth into the mark he'd made. His mate, his claim.

Joni wasn't sure her legs would hold her once Atlas pulled out of her, but they had. They finished washing up and rinsing off. Dear Goddess, the man was everything she'd dreamed a mate would be and more. Now, as she stared at herself in the mirror dressed in a pair of denim jeans, which had been distressed purposefully, and one of her favorite rock band T-shirts with her hair in a messy bun, she wondered if he felt the same. The alpha house was so much more than what she was used to with Keith and even the Mystic Wolves. The White Bear Clan were wealthy on a scale that she was sure, they'd take one look at her, and turn their noses up as if they'd stepped on something nasty.

Of course, she had money in an account her parents had no clue about, and the means to make more anywhere she decided to live. Keith and his fucking with her genetics, had made her ability to move through the inter-web like a virus, had its bonuses. Only it also had its downfalls. If she did it too much, she got nose bleeds and migraines. Which was why she hadn't told the Mystic pack about her abilities. Not that she thought Niall would use her the way Keith had, but...gah, she hated having a secret from her mate.

"What's the matter?" Atlas came up behind her, his arms sliding around her hips, pulling her back against him.

She shook her head, tears threatening to fall. "Nothing." She bit her lip. "That's a lie, which you probably know."

He nodded. "Just say whatever it is, and we'll deal with it together."

So solid, her mate. She took a deep breath. Took a leap of faith. In a quiet voice, she told him how Keith had used magic, how he'd somehow manipulated her, and how she could look at a computer, think of herself inside it and be there, surfing through it. It was how the bastard had financed all that he'd done. She hadn't been the only one, but she'd been the only survivor.

"Do you still do it? Is it a compulsion?" He turned her to face him.

She shook her head. "It's not as easy as it had been. I started getting migraines and nose bleeds even before he was killed. For the last eight months or so, I've only done it so I could build a new identity."

He put one finger under her chin, raising her face up to his. "Let's tackle this one thing at a time. First, you don't need a new identity anymore. Second, you don't need to use that ability, ever again. Third, maybe since he's dead, whatever fucked up mojo he was using is dwindling away. No matter what, we're in this together. I love you, every piece of you. Now, you ready to go face the clan?"

Her chin shook from the effort it took her not to cry. Her mate truly meant what he'd said. Maybe, just maybe, he was right. She planned to be the best mate to him. Her wolf growled inside her, letting her know she was a badass. "Let's do this," she agreed.

"My sexy mate, I don't know if I should let you walk out of here looking so fucking good. Have I told you I love your ass?" His hands caressed both cheeks.

"Let's go, bossy bear, or we'll never get out of here." She pressed her face to his chest, his steady heartbeat reassuring.

"Yo, Alpha, let's go. You got a mass of bears out in the front yard waiting for you to come out."

"Which brother was that?" Joni asked, taking a step back, her back hitting the vanity.

"That's Abyle. You'll figure them out in no time."

They walked out together, hands clasped, swinging back and forth. "If not, you think they'll be bothered if I call them Big Bear Bro One and Two, kinda like Thing One and Thing Two?"

"Don't even think about it," both men said at the same time.

Joni and Atlas walked outside with Abyle and Atika flanking them. Shauny was already on the porch wearing an outfit like what Joni had on, making her feel marginally better. She scanned the faces of the crowd, seeing shock and curiosity.

Atlas stopped them on the top step of the porch, keeping their hands together. He lifted his right hand, putting two fingers in his mouth as the murmurs from the crowd increased. His whistle was loud enough, Joni feared her poor wolf hearing might've been damaged.

"Sorry, Achwahnaja," he whispered, kissing her on the temple.

The crowd quieted, then a gasp had them parting.

Joni squealed for a whole other reason as she saw her friends Erica and Kyle, followed by Oakland walking through. Atlas kept her hand in his, letting her know she was to stay put and allow them to come to where they were. *"We are the alpha pair. They come to us,"* he said through their link.

"Did you know they were coming?" she asked, looking up at him.

"I might've made sure they had safe passage and a little help from a pink lady."

"It's good to see you both again. Erica, how're you feeling?" he asked aloud.

"What's the meaning of this?" A clan elder asked, stepping forward. The old male glared at the trio.

"Sage, these are friends who helped save my mate when Matilda and a couple dozen others from this clan and the Red River Clan tried to kill her and me." Atlas released Joni's hand, pulling her into his side.

"That's a lie. Matilda would never," Sage sputtered.

Atlas narrowed his eyes. "You and I both know I didn't lie." He recounted what had unfolded before his clan, waiting for them to quiet again. "Now, Joni is my truemate, chosen by both Goddesses. I'll give you all a choice. Accept my mate and I, or we will leave, and you can find a new alpha. Either of my brothers would fill the shoes, probably better than me."

While he spoke, Joni and Erica stepped off to the side of the porch with Kyle hovering close by. He could see the female wolf was almost completely healed thanks to Lula. He turned to face the crowd, his brothers protesting his suggestion of them taking his place. He grinned at their outrage.

"Oh shit," Shauny whispered.

He turned in time to see several female bears shifting off to the side near his mate and Erica, too close for him to reach them before they could get to Joni. Time slowed as his mate shoved Erica back a dozen feet, landing on top of Kyle, her wolf ripping out of her, the pure white beast facing off against the three female grizzlies.

"Holy fuck! What is she?" Abyle asked.

Atlas crossed his arms over his chest, watching his mate swat a grizzly female down, then bat another away before picking up another like she was a toy. He was sure she'd go on playing with the females for hours if he let her, but he was sure her point had been made. "Joni, can you quit playing with the females now? I think they've learned their lesson, yes?" He looked at the crowd of bears, most smiling at the display.

Joni backhanded the first grizzly again, like she felt the female had gotten off too easy, then trotted over to the front of the crowd. Her wolf was easily twice as big as the biggest grizzly, except his dire bear. She shifted, her outfit appearing on her without a tear. "They started it," she grumbled.

He held his hand out, waiting for her to walk up the steps to his side. "Yes, and I do believe you finished it. Anybody else want to challenge the alpha female?" He looked at the faces of his people. "Joni is a dire wolf, like I'm a dire bear, a white dire wolf, as I'm the white dire bear. What that means for this clan is this. If you want me to stay as alpha there's going to be some changes. First, we will no longer be the White Bear Clan. I'm not sure what we'll be called, but as you can see, my mate isn't a bear. My cubs might be pups."

Joni squeezed his hand. "How about The Wilder Crew? Kind of like an homage to the Wilde Crew down south? If they don't want us, we'll start our own crew and take in other lost ones like Erica and Kyle once were, like I was."

He kissed her nose, then looked out at the people he'd grown up with. The clan was significantly smaller thanks to Matilda and her crazy stunt. If they continued the way they were, living in isolation, none of them would find their truemates. The White Bear Clan needed to become something new. They needed to become the Wilder Crew in order to survive.

"I'm all for it. If you go, we go," Abyle said.

Atika walked to his other side, nodding. One by one the clan moved forward, even the three females who'd just had their asses handed to them. They'd messed with the wrong wolf, but they'd learned she was also a true alpha. She and Atlas would be what a real alpha pair was supposed to be, leading them into a future that wasn't stifling, taking but not giving. The Wilder Crew is going to destroy the White Bear Clan in order to become what they need.

"You're exactly what we needed," Shauny said, pulling Joni in for a hug.

"We'll find you a mate." Joni looked over at Atlas talking to his brothers.

Shauny pulled away, a sad smile on her face. "Go over there. He needs you."

The twins walked off, their backs stiff. Joni looked at Shauny then the twins, wishing she could fix them all. One step at a time. She wasn't the alpha bitch of the Wilder Crew for nothing. She cracked her neck, then went to Atlas's side, where she belonged. His arm slid around her, pulling her against him. "Love you, mate," she whispered.

"Love you more," he said, kissing her temple. "So, you ready to talk to your friends?" Atlas tipped his head toward the driveway.

Joni's breath caught as the doors opened on a huge SUV. One by one her friends, and their mates walked up the drive, passing the bears without pause. Sky, goddess love her, actually chest bumped one of the female bear's who'd jumped Joni.

From where she stood, she wasn't sure if she'd be able to make the huge leap in order to intervene, but whatever the bear saw in Sky's eyes kept her from retaliating. "Hey," Joni said, eyeing the group of wolves.

Taryn stopped in front of her with Jett at her back. "Hey? Really, that's all you got to say?" she growled.

Joni looked down at her friend, then over at Sky. Her heart raced. "Um, so what's brought you all the way up here?"

"Oh, my goddess. Somebody hold me back, or I'm liable to smack a...what the hell are you now?" Taryn sniffed the air.

"That is so rude, T," Sky nudged forward. "What our friend here is trying to say is—well, I guess what we wanted to know is, why the hell you left and what the hell were you thinking?" Sky's purple eyes brightened.

"I made a deal with Keith and for better or worse, I kept it," Joni said, her shoulders back, staring straight ahead. "Things were messed up inside me...because of what happened."

Atlas rubbed his head on top of hers. "If you'd like to share your story without having to talk it out, I can help," Atlas offered.

Joni took a deep breath. "No, I can do this. Long story short, I agreed to allow Keith to—let me experience what he did to you, only he didn't have to physically be there. I...I let him into my mind, and I allowed him to, well, you know, whatever T suffered I did to. In exchange, he let us care for her and allowed my parents and I to live relatively unharmed."

"What the fuck were you thinking? He could've killed you," Taryn cried, tears leaking from her eyes.

"It was the only way he'd let us help you." Joni held her hands up.

Taryn shook her head. "Bullshit, he had an agenda. He always had one, and it was never one that benefited anyone but him. Is that why...why you couldn't shift?"

Joni looked away. She didn't want to talk about the past or what she'd gone through. "It doesn't matter anymore. What's done is done. We can't change it, right?"

Sky growled, making Atlas move forward, his arms sliding around her waist. "Would you all like to come inside?"

Jett sighed. "Sorry, man. Come on, why don't we take this inside and remember, you both said you'd be nice. Besides, I'm pretty sure after seeing what she becomes, I'd keep her on our side," he teased.

"Hey, I've got some dragon in me," Sky said. "Besides, Lula's the one who told us about this little meet and greet. If shit goes down, maybe the pink dragon will come and rescue us?"

Her friends' words had them all laughing as they walked inside. Joni knew her life was forever changed. Her world was no longer going to revolve around the Mystic Wolves, but the bounds that had brought the three of them together had been forged long before she'd found her truemate. She felt a tear slide down her cheek as she realized home was no longer where she'd grown up.

"Hey, we're only a phone call, or thought away." Taryn slid her hand into Joni's, linking them.

Sky grabbed her other hand. "We may not have had the easiest of lives, or got to be as close as I'd wished, but you both have always been the sisters of my heart. Even if you move to the freaking Tundra, which by the way, this far North is going to be cold as fucking Hell, which is why I'm now calling it the Tundra, you're still my sister."

A laugh escaped her. "I have a big ass bear to keep me warm."

Taryn squeezed her fingers. "I guess you do. By the way, is it true about what they say about bears?"

Atlas lifted Joni up, pulling her away from her friends, saying over his shoulder. "Bears and all animals shit in the woods, females, it's natural in our shifts, get over it," he growled.

Joni looked over his shoulder at her friends as they walked hand-in-hand with their mates, following them into her and Atlas's home. Yeah, she had a bumpy road getting to where she was, and knew their lives had one hell of a path still to come. With the Wilder Crew there was going to be growing pains, and these were ones she couldn't wait to face with her bossy bear.

"I'll show you just how bossy I am when your friends leave," he whispered against her temple.

She wrapped her arms more securely around his neck. "You reading my mind?"

He pressed his forehead against hers. "We're connected on a level my bear and your wolf don't seem to want to stop. Can't you read mine?"

She stopped thinking about her friends to realize that, yes, she could see what he'd been thinking, and immediately wished they were alone. "You better stop that, or my friends are going to be able to smell exactly what I'm thinking."

His growl had her wolf raking at her insides. "Ah, Achwahnaja, they already know," he murmured.

The End

About Elle Boon

Elle Boon is a USA Today Bestselling Author who lives in Middle-Merica as she likes to say...with her husband and Kally Kay her black lab and writing partner. She has two amazing kids, Jazz and Goob, and is a Mi-Mi to one adorable little nugget named Romy, or maybe better known as RomyGirl, who has totally won over everyone who sees hers. She's known for saying "Bless Your Heart" and dropping lots of F-bombs, but she loves where this new journey has taken her and has no plans on stopping.

She writes what she loves to read, and that's romance, whether it's about Navy SEALs, or paranormal beings, as long as there is a happily ever after. Her biggest hope is that after readers have read one of her stories, they fall in love with her characters as much as she did. She loves creating new worlds, and has more stories just waiting to be written. Elle believes in happily ever afters, and can guarantee you will always get one with her stories.

Connect with Elle online, she loves to hear from you:

www.elleboon.com[1]

https://www.facebook.com/elle.boon

https://www.facebook.com/Elle-Boon-Author-1429718517289545/

https://twitter.com/ElleBoon1

https://www.facebook.com/groups/RacyReads/

https://www.facebook.com/groups/188924878146358/

https://www.facebook.com/groups/1405756769719931/

https://www.facebook.com/groups/wewroteyourbookboyfriends/

https://www.goodreads.com/author/show/8120085.Elle_Boon

https://www.bookbub.com/authors/elle-boon

https://www.instagram.com/elleboon/

http://www.elleboon.com/newsletter/

---

1. http://www.elleboon.com

Other Books by Elle Boon

Ravens of War
Selena's Men
Two For Tamara
Jaklyn's Saviors
Kira's Warriors

Mystic Wolves
Accidentally Wolf & His Perfect Wolf (1 Volume)
Jett's Wild Wolf
Bronx's Wounded Wolf
A Fey's Wolf
Their Wicked Wolf
Atlas's Forbidden Wolf

SmokeJumpers
FireStarter
Berserker's Rage
A SmokeJumpers Christmas
Mind Bender, Coming Soon

Iron Wolves MC
Lyric's Accidental Mate
Xan's Feisty Mate
Kellen's Tempting Mate
Slater's Enchanted Mate
Dark Lovers
Bodhi's Synful Mate
Turo's Fated Mate
Arynn's Chosen Mate
Coti's Unclaimed Mate

Miami Nights
Miami Inferno
Rescuing Miami

Standalone

Wild and Dirty

SEAL Team Phantom Series

Delta Salvation

Delta Recon

Delta Rogue

Delta Redemption

Mission Saving Shayna

Protecting Teagan

The Dark Legacy Series

Dark Embrace

Royal Sons MC

Royally Twisted, Book 1

Found in Because He's Perfect anthology

Printed in Great Britain
by Amazon